James Grant

Under the Red Dragon

A novel. Part 1

James Grant

Under the Red Dragon
A novel. Part 1

ISBN/EAN: 9783337065584

Printed in Europe, USA, Canada, Australia, Japan

Cover: Foto ©Andreas Hilbeck / pixelio.de

More available books at **www.hansebooks.com**

UNDER THE RED DRAGON.

A Novel.

By JAMES GRANT,

AUTHOR OF 'THE ROMANCE OF WAR,' 'ONLY AN ENSIGN,' ETC.

IN THREE VOLUMES.

VOL. I.

LONDON:

TINSLEY BROTHERS, 18 CATHERINE ST. STRAND.

1872.

CONTENTS OF VOL. I.

UNDER THE RED DRAGON.

CHAPTER I.

THE INVITATION.

'AND *she* is to be there—nay, is there already; so
one more chance is given me to meet her. But
for what ?—to part again silently, and more helplessly bewitched than ever, perhaps. Ah, never
will she learn to love me as I love her !' thought I,
as I turned over my old friend's letter, not venturing, however, to give utterance to this aloud, as
the quizzical eyes of Phil Caradoc were upon me.

'A penny for your thoughts, friend Harry ?'
said he, laughing ; 'try another cigar, and rouse
yourself. What the deuce is in this letter, that it
affects you so ? Have you put a pot of money on
the wrong horse ?'

'Been jilted, had a bill returned, or what?' suggested Gwynne.

'Neither, fortunately,' said I; 'it is simply an invitation from Sir Madoc Lloyd, which rather perplexes me.'

At this time our regiment was then in the East, awaiting with the rest of the army some movement to be made from Varna, either towards Bessarabia or the Crimea—men's minds were undecided as to which, while her Majesty's Ministers seemed to have no thought on the subject. Our dépôt belonged to the provisional battalion at Winchester, where Caradoc, Gwynne, two other subalterns, and I, with some two hundred rank and file, expected ere long the fiat of the fates who reign at the Horse Guards to send us forth to win our laurels from the Russians, or, what seemed more probable, a grave where the pest was then decimating our hapless army, in the beautiful but perilous vale of Aladdyn, on the coast of Bulgaria.

We had just adjourned from mess, to have a quiet cheroot and glass of brandy-and-water in my quarters, when I received from my man, Owen Evans, the letter the contents of which awakened so many new hopes and tantalising wishes in my heart, and on which so much of my fate in the future might hinge.

The bare, half-empty, or but partially-furnished single room accorded by the barrack authorities to me as a subaltern, in that huge square edifice built of old by Charles II. for a royal residence, seemed by its aspect but little calculated to flatter the brilliant hopes in question. Though ample in size, it was far from regal in its appurtenances—the barrack furniture, a camp-bed, my baggage trunks piled in one corner, swords and a gun case in another, books, empty bottles, cigar-boxes, and a few pairs of boots ostentatiously displayed in a row by Evans, making up its entire garniture, and by very contrast in its meagreness compelling me to smile sadly at myself for the ambitious ideas the letter of my old friend had suggested; and thus, for a minute or so ignoring, or rather oblivious of, the presence of my two companions, my eye wandered dreamily over the far-extended mass of old brick houses and the gray church towers of the city, all visible from the open window, and then steeped in the silver haze of the moonlight.

Sipping their brandy-and-water, each with a lighted cheroot between his fingers, their shell-jackets open, and their feet unceremoniously planted on a hard wooden chair, while they lounged back upon another, were Phil Caradoc and Charley Gwynne. The first a good specimen of a handsome, curly-haired, and heedless young Englishman, who shot, fished, hunted, pulled a steady oar, and could keep his wicket against any man, while shining without effort in almost every manly sport, was moreover a finished gentleman and thorough good fellow.

Less fashionable in appearance and less dashing in manner, though by no means less soldierlike, Gwynne was his senior by some ten years. He was more grave and thoughtful, for he had seen more of the service and more of the world. Already a gray hair or so had begun to mingle with the blackness of his heavy moustache, and the lines of thought were traceable on his forehead and about the corners of his keen dark-gray eyes; for he was a hard-working officer, who had been promoted from the ranks when the regiment lay at Barbadoes, and was every inch a soldier. And now they sat opposite me, waiting, with a half-comical expression, for farther information as to their queries; and though we were great friends, and usually had few secrets from each other, I began to find that I had *one* now, and that a little reticence was necessary.

'You know Sir Madoc's place in North Wales?' said I.

'Of course,' replied Caradoc; 'there are few of ours who don't. Half the regiment have been there as visitors at one time or other.'

'Well, he wishes me to get leave between returns—for even longer if I can—and run down there for a few weeks. ". Come early, if possible," he adds; " the girls insist on having an outdoor fête, and a lot of nice folks are coming. Winny has arranged that we shall have a regimental band—the Yeomanry one too, probably; then we are to have a Welsh harper, of course, and an itinerant Merlin in the grotto, to tell every one's fortune, and to predict your promotion and the C.B., if the seer remains sober. While I write, little Dora is drawing up a programme of the dances, and marking off, she says, those which she means to have with *you*."'

Here I paused; but seeing they expected to

hear more, for the writer was a friend of us all, I read on coolly, and with an air of as much unconsciousness as I could assume :

' " Lady Estelle Cressingham is with us—by the way, she seems to know you, and would, I think, like to see more of you.   She is a very fine girl, though not pure Welsh ; but that she cannot help—it is her misfortune, not her fault.   We have also a fellow here, though I don't quite know how he got introduced—Hawkesby Guilfoyle, who met her abroad at Ems, or Baden-Baden, or one of those places where one meets everybody, and he seems uncommonly attentive—so much so, that I wonder her mother permits it ; but he seems to have some special power or influence over the old lady, though his name is not as yet, or ever likely to be, chronicled by Burke or Debrett.   In lieu of the goat which your regiment lost in Barbadoes, Winifred has a beautiful pet one, a magnificent animal, which she means to present to the Welsh Fusileers.   Tell them so.   And now, for yourself, I will take no refusal, and Winny and Dora will take none either ; so pack your traps, and come off so soon as you can get leave.   You need not, unless you choose, bring horses ; we have plenty of cavalry here. Hope you will be able to stay till the 12th, and have a shot at the grouse. Meanwhile, believe me, my dear Hardinge, yours, &c., MADOC MERE-DYTH LLOYD." '

'Kindly written, and so like the jolly style of the old Baronet,' said Gwynne. 'I have ridden with him once or twice in the hunting-field—on a borrowed mount, of course,' added poor Charley, who had only his pay, and, being an enthusiast in his profession, was no lounger in the service.

'But what is there in all this that perplexes you?' asked Caradoc, who, I suppose, had been attentively observing me. As he spoke, I coloured visibly, feeling the while that I did so.

'The difficulty about leave, perhaps,' I stammered.

'You'll go, of course,' said Caradoc. 'His place—Craigaderyn Court—is one of the finest in North Wales; his daughters are indeed charming; and you are certain to meet only people of the best style there.'

'Yet he seems to doubt this—what is his name?—Guilfoyle, however,' said I.

'What of that? One swallow—you know the

adage. I should go, if I had the invitation. His eldest daughter has, I have heard, in her own right, no end of coal-mines somewhere, and many grassy acres of dairy farms in the happy hunting-grounds of the midland counties.'

'By Jove!' murmured Gwynne, as he lit a fresh cigar; 'she should be the girl for me.'

'But I have another inducement than even the fair Winny,' said I.

'Oho! Lady—'

'Sir Madoc,' said I hastily, 'is an old friend of my family, and having known me from infancy, he almost views me as a son. Don't mistake me,' I added, reddening with positive annoyance at the hearty laugh my admission elicited; 'Miss Lloyd and I are old friends too, and know each other a deuced deal too well to tempt the perils of matrimony together. We have no draughts ready for the East, nor will there be yet awhile; even our last recruits are not quite licked into shape.'

'No,' sighed Gwynne, who had a special charge of the said 'licking into shape.'

'And so, as the spring drills are over, I shall try my luck with old R—.'

The person thus bluntly spoken of was the

lieutenant-colonel of the dépôt battalion — one who kept a pretty tight hand over us all in general, and the subalterns in particular.

'Stay,' I exclaimed suddenly ; 'here is a postscript. "Bring Caradoc of yours with you, and Gwynne, too, if you can. Winny has mastered the duet the former sent her, and is anxious to try it over with him." '

'Caradoc will only be too happy, if the genius who presides over us in the orderly-room is propitious,' said Phil, colouring and laughing.

'Thank Sir Madoc for me, old fellow,' said Gwynne half sadly. 'Tell him that the Fates have made me musketry instructor, and that daily I have that

> "Delightful task ! to rear the tender thought,
> To teach the young idea how to *shoot*"—

to set up Taffy and Giles Chawbacon in the Hythe position, and drill them to fire without closing both eyes and blazing in the air.'

' "In the lawn," adds Sir Madoc, "we are to have everything—from waltzing to croquet (which, being an old fellow, and being above insteps and and all that sort of thing, I think the slowest

game known), and from cliquot and sparkling
hock to bottled stout and bitter beer—unlimited
flirtation too, according to that wag, Dora."'

'A tempting bill of fare, especially with two
such hostesses,' said Gwynne; 'but for me to quit
Winchester is impossible. Even the stale dodge
of "urgent private affairs" won't serve me. Such
droll ideas of the service old Sir Madoc must have,
to think that three of us could leave the dépôt,
and all at once, too!'

'I shall try my luck, however.'

'And I too,' rejoined Caradoc. 'I am entitled
to leave. Price of ours will take my guards for
me. Wales will be glorious in this hot month.
I *did* all the dear old Principality last year—went
over every foot of Snowdonia, leaving nothing undone, from singing "Jenny Jones" to dancing a
Welsh jig at a harvest-home.'

'But you didn't go over Snowdonia with such
a girl as Winifred Lloyd?'

'No, certainly,' said he, laughing, and almost
reddening again. 'Nature, even in my native
Wales, must be more charming under such bright
auspices and happy influence. So Wales be it, if
possible. London, of course, is empty just now,

and all who can get out of it will be yachting at
Cowes, shooting in Scotland, fishing in Norway,
backing the red at Baden-Baden, climbing the
Matterhorn, or, it may be, the Peter Botte; killing
buffaloes in America, or voyaging up the Nile in
canoes. Rotten-row will be a desert, the opera a
place of silence and cobwebs; and the irresistible
desire to go somewhere and be doing something,
no matter what, which inspires all young Britons
about this time, renders Sir Madoc's invitation
most tempting and acceptable.'

'Till the route comes for the East,' said I.

'Potting the Ruskies, and turning my musketry theory into practice, are likely to be my chief
relaxations and excitement,' said Gwynne, with a
good-natured laugh, as he applied his hand to the
brandy-bottle. 'At present I have other work in
hand than flirting with countesses, or visiting
heiresses. But I envy you both, and heartily
wish you all pleasure,' he added, as he shook
hands and left us early, as he had several squads
to put through that most monotonous of all drill
(shot drill perhaps excepted)—a course of musketry—betimes in the morning.

We knew that Gwynne, who was a tall, thin,

close-flanked, and square-shouldered, but soldier-like fellow, had nothing but his pay; and having a mother to support, he was fain to slave as a musketry instructor, the five shillings extra daily being a great pecuniary object to him. He was very modest withal, and feared that, nathless his red coat and stalwart figure, his chances of an heiress, even in Cottonopolis, were somewhat slender.

CHAPTER II.

THE MOTH AND THE CANDLE.

PHILIP CARADOC, perceiving that I was somewhat dull and disposed to indulge in reverie, soon retired also, and we separated, intending to mature our plans after morning parade next day, as I knew that secretly Caradoc was very much attached to Winifred Lloyd, though that young lady by no means reciprocated his affection. But I, seized by an irresistible impulse, could not wait for our appointed time; so, the moment he was gone, I opened my desk, wrote my application for leave, and desiring Evans to take it to the orderly-room among his first duties on the morrow, threw open a second window to admit the soft breeze of the summer night, lit another cigar, and sat down to indulge in the train of thought Sir Madoc's unexpected letter had awakened within my breast.

Yet I was not much given to reflection — far from it, perhaps; and it is lucky for soldiers that they rarely indulge much in thought, or that the system of their life is apt to preclude time or opportunity for it.

I had come home on a year's sick-leave from the West Indies, where the baleful night-dews, and a fever caught in the rainy season, had nearly finished my career while stationed at Up Park Camp; and now, through the friendly interest of Sir Madoc, I had been gazetted to the Welsh Fusileers, as I preferred the chances of the coming war and military service in any part of Europe to broiling uselessly in the land of the Maroons.

Our army was in the East, I have said, encamped in the vale of Aladdyn, between Varna and the sea. There camp-fever and the terrible cholera were filling fast with graves the grassy plain and all the Valley of the Plague, as the Bulgarians so aptly named it; and though I was not sorry to escape the perils encountered where no honour could be won, I was pretty weary of the daily round at Winchester, of barrack life, of in-lying pickets, guards, parades, and drill. I had been seven years in the service, and deemed myself somewhat of a veteran, though only five-and-twenty. I was weary too of belonging to a provisional battalion, wherein, beyond the narrow circle of one's own dépôt, no two men have the slightest interest in each other, or seem to care if they ever meet again, the whole organisation being temporary, and where the duties of such a battalion—it being, in effect, a strict military school for training recruits—are harassing to the newly-fledged, and a dreadful bore to the fully-initiated, soldier.

So, till the time came when the order would be, 'Eastward, ho!' Sir Madoc had opportunely offered me a little relaxation and escape from all this; and though he knew it not, his letter might be perhaps the means of doing much more—of opening up a path to happiness and fortune, or leaving one closed for ever behind me in sorrow, mortification, and bitterness of heart.

Good old Sir Madoc (or, as he loved to call himself, Madoc ap Meredyth Lloyd) had in his youth been an unsuccessful lover of my mother, then the pretty Mary Vassal, a belle in her second season; and now, though she had long since passed away, he had a strong regard for me. For her sake he had a deep and kindly interest in my welfare; and as he had no son (no heir to his baronetcy, with all its old traditional honours), he quite regarded me in the light of one; and having two daughters, desired nothing more than that I should cut the service and become one in reality. So many an act of friendship and many a piece of stamped paper he had done for me, when, in the first years of my career, I got into scrapes with rogues upon the turf, at billiards, and with those curses of all barracks, the children of Judea.

Had I seen where my own good fortune really lay, I should have fallen readily into the snare so temptingly baited for me, a halfpennyless sub.; for Winifred Lloyd was a girl among a thousand, so far as brilliant attractions go, and, moreover, was not indisposed to view me favourably (at least, so my vanity taught me). But this world is full of cross purposes; people are too often blind to their profit and advantage, and, as Jaques has it, ' thereby hangs a tale.'

All the attractions of bright-eyed Winny Lloyd, personal and pecuniary, were at that time as nothing to me. I had casually, when idling in London, been introduced to, and had met at several places, this identical Lady Cressingham, whom my friend had mentioned so incidentally and in such an off-hand way in his letter ; and that sentence it was which brought the blood to my temples and quickened all the pulses of my heart.

She was very beautiful—as the reader will find when we meet her by and by — and I had soon learned to love her, but without quite venturing to say so ; to love her as much as it was possible for one without hope of ultimate success, and so circumstanced as I was—a poor gentleman, with little more in the world save my sword and epaulettes. Doubtless she had seen and read the emotion with which she had inspired me, for women have keen perceptions in such matters ; and though it seems as if it was on her very smile that the mainspring of my existence turned, the whole affair might be but a source of quiet amusement, of curiosity, or gratified vanity to her.

Yet, by every opportunity that the chances and artificial system of society in town afforded, I had evinced this passion, the boldness of which my secret heart confessed.

Her portrait, a stately full-length, was in the

Academy, and how often had I gazed at it, till in fancy the limner's work seemed to become instinct with life !   Traced on the canvas by no unskilful hand, it seemed to express a somewhat haughty consciousness of her own brilliant beauty, and somehow I fancied a deuced deal more of her own exalted *position*, as the only daughter of a deceased but wealthy peer, and as if she rather disdained alike the criticism and the admiration of the crowd of middle-class folks who thronged the Academy halls.

Visions of her — as I had seen her in the Countess's curtained box at the opera, her rare and high-class beauty enhanced by all the accessories of fashion and costume, by brilliance of light and the subtle flash of many a gem amid her hair ; when galloping along the Row on her beautiful satin-skinned bay ; or while driving after in the Park, with all those appliances and surroundings that wealth and rank confer—came floating before me, with the memory of words half uttered, and glances responded to when eye met eye, and told so much more than the tongue might venture to utter.

Was it mere vanity, or reality, that made me

think her smile *had* brightened when she met me, or that when I rode by her side she preferred me to the many others who daily pressed forward to greet her amid that wonderful place, the Row? Her rank, and the fact that she was an heiress, had no real weight with me; nor did these fortuitous circumstances enhance her merit in my eyes, though they certainly added to the difficulty of winning her. Was it possible that the days of disinterested and romantic love, like those of chivalry, were indeed past—gone with the days when

> ' It was a clerk's son, of low degree,
> Loved the king's daughter of Hongarie'?

With the love that struggled against humble fortune in my heart, I had that keenly sensitive pride which is based on proper self-respect. Hope I seemed to have none. What hope could I, Harry Hardinge, a mere subaltern, with little more than seven-and-sixpence per diem, have of obtaining such a wife as Lady Estelle Cressingham, and, more than all, of winning the good wishes of her over-awing mamma?

Though 'love will venture in when it daurna weel be seen,' I could neither be hanged nor reduced to the ranks for my presumption, like the luckless Captain Ogilvie; who, according to the Scottish ballad, loved the Duke of Gordon's bonnie daughter Jean. Yet defeat and rejection might cover me with certain ridicule, leaving the stings of wounded self-esteem to rankle all the deeper, by thrusting the partial disparity of our relative positions in society more unpleasantly and humiliatingly before me and the world; for there is a snobbery in rank that is only equalled by the snobbery of wealth, and here I might have both to encounter. And so, as I brooded over these things, some very levelling and rather democratic, if not entirely Communal, ideas began to occur to me.

And yet, for the Countess and those who set store upon such empty facts, I could have proved my descent from Nicholas Hardinge, knight, of King's Newton in Derbyshire; who in the time of Henry VII. held his lands by the homely and most sanitary tenure of furnishing clean straw for his Majesty's bed when he and his queen, Elizabeth of York, passed that way, together with fresh rushes from the margin of the Trent wherewith to strew the floor of the royal apartment. But this would seem as yesterday to the fair Estelle, who boasted of an ancestor one Sir Hugh Cressingham, who, as history tells us, was defeated and *flayed* by the Scots after the battle of Stirling; while old Sir Madoc Lloyd, who doubtless traced himself up to Noah ap Lamech, would have laughed both pedigrees to scorn.

Leaving London, I had striven to stifle as simply absurd the passion that had grown within me, and had joined at Winchester in the honest and earnest hope that ere long the coming campaign would teach me to forget the fair face and witching eyes, and, more than all, the winning manner that haunted me ; and now I was to be cast within their magic influence once more, and doubtless to be hopelessly lost.

To have acted wisely, I should have declined the invitation and pleaded military duty ; yet to see her once, to be with her once again, without that cordon of guardsmen and cavaliers who daily formed her mounted escort in Rotten-row, and with all the chances our quiet mutual residence in a sequestered country mansion, when backed by all the influence and friendship of Sir Madoc, must afford me, proved a temptation too strong for resistance or for my philosophy; so, like the poor moth, infatuated and self-doomed, I resolved once more to rush at the light which dazzled me.

'She seems to know you, *and would like to see more of you,*' ran the letter of Sir Madoc. I read that line over and over again, studying it minutely in every way. Were those dozen words simply the embodiment of his own ideas, or were they her personally expressed wish put literally into writing? Were they but the reflex of some casual remark? Even that conviction would bring me happiness. And so, after my friends left me, I sat pondering thus, blowing long rings of concentric smoke in the moonlight; and on those words of Sir Madoc raising not only a vast and aerial castle, but a 'bower of bliss,' as the pantomimes have it at Christmas time.

But how about this Mr. Hawkesby Guilfoyle? was my next thought. Could *his* attentions be tolerated by such a stately and watchful dowager as the Countess of Naseby? Could Sir Madoc actually hint that such as he might have a chance of success, when I had none? The idea was too ridiculous; for I had heard whispers of this man before, in London and about the clubs, where he was generally deemed to be a species of adventurer, the exact source of whose revenue no one knew. One fact was pretty certain : he was unpleasantly successful at billiards and on the turf.

If he—to use his own phraseology—was daring enough to enter stakes for such a prize as Lord Cressingham's daughter, why should not I ?

Thus, in reverie of a somewhat chequered kind, I lingered on, while the shadows of the cathedral, its lofty tower and choir, the spire of St. Lawrence, and many other bold features of the view began to deepen or become more uncertain on the city roofs below, and from amid which their masses stood upward in a flood of silver sheen.

Ere long the full-orbed moon—that seemed to float in beauty beneath its snow-white clouds, looking calmly down on Winchester, even as she had done ages ago, ere London was a capital, and when the white city was the seat of England's Saxon, Danish, and Norman dynasties, of Alfred's triumphs and Canute's glories — began at last to pale and wane ; and the solemn silence of the morning—for dewy morning it was now—was broken only by the chime of the city bells and clocks, and by the tread of feet in the gravelled barrack-yard, as the reliefs went round, and the sentinels were changed.

The first red streak of dawn was beginning to steal across the east; the bugles were pealing reveilles, waking all the hitherto silent echoes of the square; and just about the time when worthy and unambitious Charley Gwynne would be parading his first squad for 'aiming drill' at sundry bull's-eyes painted on the barrack-walls, I retired to dream over a possible future, and to hope that if the stars were propitious, at the altar of that somewhat dingy fane, St. George's, Hanover-square, I might yet become the son-in-law of the late Earl of Naseby, Baron Cressingham of Cotteswold, in the county of Northampton, and of Walcot Park in Hants, Lord-lieutenant, *custos rotulorum*, and so forth, as I had frequently and secretly read in the mess-room copy of Sir Bernard Burke's thick royal octavo; 'the Englishman's Bible' according to Thackeray, and, as I greatly feared, the somewhat exclusive *libro d' oro* of Mamma Cressingham, who was apt to reverence it pretty much as the Venetian nobles did the remarkable volume of that name.

CHAPTER III.

LEAVE granted, our acceptance of Sir Madoc's invitation duly telegraphed—'wired,' as the phrase
is now—our uniforms doffed and mufti substituted,
the morning of the second day ensuing saw Caradoc and myself on the Birmingham railway *en
route* for Chester; the exclusive occupants of a
softly cushioned compartment, where, by the influence of a couple of florins slipped deftly and
judiciously into the palm of an apparently unconscious and incorruptible official, we could lounge
at our ease, and enjoy without intrusion the *Times*,
Punch, or our own thoughts, and the inevitable
cigar.

Though in mufti we had uniform with us; we
believed in it then, and in its influence; for certain
German ideas of military tailoring subsequent to
the Crimean war had not shorn us of our epau-

lettes, and otherwise reduced the character of our regimentals to something akin to the livery of a penny postman or a railway guard.

Somehow, I felt more hopeful of my prospects, when, with the bright sunshine of July around us, I found myself spinning at the rate of fifty miles per hour by the express train—the motion was almost as imperceptible as the speed was exhilarating—and swiftly passed the scenes on either side, the broad green fields of growing grain, the grassy paddocks, the village churches, the snug and picturesque homesteads of Warwick and Worcestershire.

We glided past Rugby, where Caradoc had erewhile conned his tasks in that great Elizabethan pile which is built of white brick with stone angles and cornices, and where in the playing fields he had gallantly learned to keep his wicket with that skill which made him our prime regimental bat and bowler too. Coventry next, where of course we laughed as we thought of 'peeping Tom' and Earl Leofric's pretty countess, when we saw its beautiful and tapering spires rise over the dark and narrow streets below. Anon, we paused amid the busy but grimy world of Bir-

mingham, which furnishes half the world with the
implements of destruction ; Stafford, with its
ruined castle on a well-wooded eminence ; and ere
long we halted in quaint old Chester by the Dee,
where the stately red stone tower of the cathedral
rises darkly over its picturesque thoroughfares of
the middle ages.

There the rail went no farther then ; but a
carriage sent by Sir Madoc awaited us at the sta-
tion, and we had before us the prospect of a
delightful drive for nearly thirty miles amid the
beautiful Welsh hills ere we reached his residence.

' This whiff of the country is indeed delightful !' exclaimed Caradoc, as we bowled along on a
lovely July evening, the changing shadows of the
rounded hills deepening as the sun verged westward ; ' it makes one half inclined to cut the
service, and turn farmer or cattle-breeding squire
—even to chuck ambition, glory, and oneself away
upon a landed heiress, if such could be found
ready to hand.'

' Even upon Winifred Lloyd, with her dairy-
farms in the midland counties, eh ?'

Phil coloured a little, but laughed good-
humouredly as he replied,

'Well, I must confess that she is somewhat more than my weakness—at present.'

At Aber-something we found a relay of fresh horses, sent on by Sir Madoc, awaiting us, the Welsh roads not being quite so smooth as a billiard-table ; and there certain hoarse gurgling expletives, uttered by ostlers and stable-boys, might have warned us that we were in the land of Owen and Hughes, Griffiths and Davies, and all the men of the Twelve Royal Tribes, even if there had not been the green mountains towering into the blue sky, and the pretty little ivy-covered inn, at the porch of which sat a white-haired harper (on the watch for patrons and customers), performing the invariable 'Jenny Jones' or *Ar-hyd-y-nos* (the live-long night), and all the while keeping a sharp Celtic eye to the expected coin.

Everything around us indicated that we were drawing nearer to the abode of Sir Madoc, and that ere long—in an hour or so, perhaps—I should again see one who, by *name* as well as circumstance, was a star that I feared and hoped would greatly influence all my future. The Eastern war, and, more than all, the novelty of any war after forty years of European peace, occupied keenly the minds of all thinking people. My regiment was already gone, and I certainly should soon have to follow it. I knew that, individually and collectively, all bound for the seat of the coming strife had a romantic and even melancholy interest, in the hearts of women especially; and I was not without some hope that this sentiment might add to my chances of finding favour with the rather haughty Estelle Cressingham.

It was a glorious summer evening when our open barouche swept along the white dusty road that wound by the base of Mynedd Hiraethrog, that wild and bleak mountain chain which rises between the Dee and its tributaries the Elwey and the Aled. Westward in the distance towered blue Snowdon, above the white floating clouds of mist, with all its subordinate peaks. In the immediate foreground were a series of beautiful hills that were glowing, and, to the eye, apparently vibrating, under a burning sunset. The Welsh woods were in all the wealth of their thickest foliage—the umbrageous growth of centuries; and where the boughs cast their deepest shadows, the dun deer and the fleet hare lurked among the fragrant fern, and the yellow sunlight fell in golden patches on the passing runnel, that leaped flashing from rock to rock, to mingle with the Alwen, or crept slowly and stealthily under the long rank grass towards Llyn-Aled.

That other accessories might not be wanting to remind us that we were in the land of the Cymri, we passed occasionally the *Carneddau,* or heaps of stones that mark the old places of battle or burial; and perched high on the hills the *Hafodtai* or summer farms, where enormous flocks of sheep—the boasted Welsh mutton—were pasturing. Then we heard at times the melancholy sound of the horn, by which inmates summon the shepherds to their meals, and the notes of which, when waking the echoes of the silent glen, have an effect so weird and mournful.

'By Jove, but we have a change here, Phil,' said I, 'a striking change indeed, from the hot and dusty gravelled yard of Winchester barracks, the awkward squads at incessant drill with dumb-bell, club, or musket; the pipeclay, the pacing-stick, and the tap of the drum!'

Through a mossgrown gateway, the design of Inigo Jones, we turned down the long straight avenue of limes that leads to Craigaderyn; a fine old mansion situated in a species of valley, its broad lawn overlooked by the identical craig from which it takes its name, 'the Rock of Birds,' a lofty and insulated mass, the resort of innumerable hawks, wood-pigeons, and even of hoarse-croaking cormorants from the cliffs about Orme's Head and Llandulas. On its summit are the ruins of an ancient British fort, wherein Sir Jorwerth Goch (*i. e.* Red Edward) Lloyd of Craigaderyn had exterminated a band of Rumpers and Roundheads in the last year of Charles I., using as a war-cry the old Welsh shout of 'Liberty, loyalty, and the long head of hair !'

On either side of the way spread the lawn, closely shorn and carefully rolled, the turf being like velvet of emerald greenness, having broad winding carriage-ways laid with gravel, the bright red of which contrasted so strongly with the verdant hue of the grass. The foliage of the timber was heavy and leafy, and there, at times, could be seen the lively squirrel leaping from branch to branch of some ancient oak, in the hollow of which lay its winter store of nuts ; the rabbit bounding across the path, from root to fern tuft; and the *bela-goed*, or yellow-breasted martin (still a denizen of the old Welsh woods), with rounded ears and sharp white claws, the terror of the poultry-yard, appeared occasionally, despite the game-keeper's gun. In one place a herd of deer were browsing near the half-leafless ruins of a mighty oak—one so old, that Owen Glendower had once reconnoitred an English force from amid its branches.

We had barely turned into the avenue, when a gentleman and two ladies, all mounted, came galloping from a side path to meet us. He and one of his companions cleared the wire fence in excellent style by a flying leap; but the other, who was less pretentiously mounted, adroitly opened the iron gate with the handle of her riding switch, and came a few paces after them to meet us. They proved to be Sir Madoc and his two daughters, Winifred and Dora.

'True to time, "by Shrewsbury clock"!' said he, cantering up; 'welcome to Craigaderyn, gentlemen! We were just looking for you.'

He was a fine hale-looking man, about sixty years old, with a ruddy complexion, and a keen, clear, dark eye; his hair, once of raven blackness, was white as silver now, though very curly or wavy still; his eyebrows were bushy and yet dark as when in youth. He was a Welsh gentleman, full of many local prejudices and sympathies; a man of the old school—for such a school has existed in all ages, and still exists even in ours of rapid progress, scientific marvels, and money-making. His manners were easy and polished, yet without anything either of style or fashion about them; for he was simple in all his tastes and ways, and was almost as plainly attired as one of his own farmers.

His figure and costume, his rubicund face, round merry eyes, and series of chins, his amplitude of paunch and stunted figure, his bottle-green coat rather short in the skirts, his deep waistcoat and low-crowned hat, were all somewhat Pickwickian in their character and *tout-ensemble*, save that in lieu of the tights and gaiters of our old friend he wore white corded breeches, and orthodox dun-coloured top-boots with silver spurs, and instead of green goggles had a gold eye-glass dangling at the end of a black-silk ribbon. Strong riding-gloves and a heavy hammer-headed whip completed his attire.

'Glad to see you, Harry, and you too, Mr.

Caradoc,' resumed Sir Madoc, who was fond of
remembering that which Phil—more a man of the
world—was apt to forget or to set little store on—
that he was descended from Sir Matthew Caradoc,
who in the days of Perkin Warbeck (an epoch but
as yesterday in Sir Madoc's estimation) was chan-
cellor of Glamorgan and steward of Gower and
Helvie; for what true Welshman is without a
pedigree? 'Let me look at you again, Harry.
God bless me! is it possible that you, a tall fellow
with a black moustache, can be the curly fair-
haired boy I have so often carried on my back and
saddle-bow, and taught to make flies of red spin-
ner and drakes' wings, when we trouted together
at Llyn Cwellyn among the hills yonder?'

'I think, papa, you would be more surprised if
you found him a curly-pated boy still,' said Miss
Lloyd.

'And it is seven years since he joined the service; what a fine fellow he has grown!'

'Papa, you are quite making Mr. Hardinge
blush!' said Dora, laughing.

'Almost at the top of the lieutenants, too;
there is luck for you!' he continued.

'More luck than merit, perhaps; more the

Varna fever than either, Sir Madoc,' said I, as he slowly relinquished my hand, which he had held for a few seconds in his, while looking kindly and earnestly into my face.

It was well browned by the sun and sea of the Windward Isles, tolerably well whiskered and moustached too; so I fear that if the good old gentleman was seeking for some resemblance to the sweet Mary Vassal of the past times, he sought in vain.

Our horses were all walking now; Sir Madoc rode on one side of the barouche, and his two daughters on the other.

'You saw my girls last season in town,' said he; 'but when you were last here, Winifred was in her first long frock, and Dora little more than a baby.'

'But Craigaderyn is all unchanged, though *we* may be,' said Winifred, whose remark had some secret point in it so far as referred to me.

'And Wales is unchanged too,' added Dora; 'Mr. Hardinge will find the odious hat of the women still lingers in the more savage regions; the itinerant harper and the goat too are not out of fashion; and we still wear our leek on the first of March.'

'And long may all this be so!' said her father, 'for since those pestilent railways have come up by Shrewsbury and Chester, with their tides of tourists, greed, dissipation, and idleness are on the increase, and all our good old Welsh customs are going to Caerphilly and the devil! Without the wants of over-civilisation we were contented; but now—*Gwell y chydig gan rad, na llawr gan avrard*,' he added with something like an angry sigh, quoting a Welsh proverb to the effect that a little with a blessing is better than much with prodigality.

CHAPTER IV.

WINNY AND DORA LLOYD.

BOTH girls were very handsome, and for their pure and brilliant complexion were doubtless indebted to the healthful breeze that swept the green sides of the Denbigh hills, together with an occasional *soupçon* of that which comes from the waters of the Irish Sea.

It is difficult to say whether Winifred could be pronounced a brunette or a blonde, her skin was so exquisitely fair, while her splendid hair was a shade of the deepest brown, and her glorious sparkling eyes were of the darkest violet blue. Their normal expression was quiet and subdued; they only flashed up at times, and she was a girl that somehow every colour became. In pure white one might have thought her lovely, and lovelier still, perhaps, in black or blue or rose, or any other tint or shade. Her fine lithe figure appeared to perfection in her close-fitting habit of dark-blue cloth, and the masses of her hair being tightly bound up under her hat, revealed the contour of her slender neck and delicately formed ear.

Dora was a smaller and younger edition of her sister—more girlish and more of a hoyden, with her lighter tresses, half golden in hue, floating loose over her shoulders and to beneath her waist from under a smart little hat, the feather and fashion of which imparted intense piquancy to the character of her somewhat irregular but remarkably pretty face and—we must admit it—rather *retroussé* nose.

Pride and a little reserve were rather the predominant style of the elder and dark-eyed sister; merriment, fun, and rather noisy flirtation were that of Dora, who permitted herself to laugh at times when her sister would barely have smiled, and to say things on which the other would never have ventured; but this *espièglerie* and a certain bearing of almost rantipole—if one may use such a term—were thought to become her.

Winifred rode a tall wiry nag, a hand or two higher than her father's stout active hunter; but

Dora preferred to scamper about on a beautiful Welsh pony, the small head, high withers, flat legs, and round hoofs of which it no doubt inherited, as Sir Madoc would have said, from the celebrated horse Merlin.

'Hope you'll stay with us till the twelfth of next month,' said he. 'The grouse are looking well.'

'Our time is doubtful, our short leave conditional, Sir Madoc,' replied Phil Caradoc, who, however, was not looking at the Baronet, but at Winifred, in the hope that the alleged brevity of his visit might find him some tender interest in her eyes, or stir some chord by its suggestiveness in her breast; but Winny, indifferent apparently to separation and danger so far as he was concerned, seemed intent on twirling the silky mane of her horse with the lash of her whip.

'Then, in about a fortnight after, we shall be blazing at the partridges,' resumed Sir Madoc, to tempt us. 'But matters are looking ill for the pheasants in October, for the gamekeeper tells me that the gapes have been prevalent among them. The poults were hatched early, and the wet weather from the mountains has made more havoc than our guns are likely to do.'

'Long before that time, Sir Madoc, I hope we shall be making havoc among the Russians,' replied Phil, still glancing covertly at Miss Lloyd.

'Ah, I hope not!' said she, roused apparently this time. 'I look forward to this most useless war with horror and dismay. So many dear friends have gone, so many more are going, it makes one quite sad! O, I shall never forget that morning in London when the poor Guards marched!'

This was addressed, not to Phil Caradoc, but to *me*.

'We knew that we should meet you,' said she, colouring, and adding a little hastily, 'We asked Lady Estelle to accompany us; but—'

'She is far too—what shall I call it?—aristocratic or unimpressionable to think of going to meet any one,' interrupted her sister.

'Don't say so, Dora! Yet I thought the loveliness of the evening would have tempted her. And Bob Spurrit the groom has broken a new pad expressly for her, by riding it for weeks with a skirt.'

So there was no temptation but 'the loveliness of the evening,' thought I; while Dora said,

'But she preferred playing over to Mr. Guilfoyle that piece of German music he gave her yesterday.'

All this was not encouraging. She knew that I was coming—a friend in whom she could not help having, from the past, rather more than a common interest—and yet she had declined to accompany those frank and kindly girls. Worse than all, perhaps she had at that moment this Mr. Hawkesby Guilfoyle hanging over her admiringly at the piano, while she played *his* music, presented to her doubtless with some suggestive, secret or implied, meaning in the sentiment or the title of it.

Jealousy readily suggested much of this, and a great deal more. That Lady Estelle was at Craigaderyn Court had been my prevailing idea when accepting so readily my kind friend's invitation. Then I should see her in a very little time now! I had been resolved to watch well how she received me, though it would be no easy task to read the secret thoughts of one so well and so carefully trained to keep all human emotions under perfect control, outwardly at least—a 'Belgravian thoroughbred,' as I once heard Sir

Madoc term her; but if she changed colour, however faintly, if there was the slightest perceptible
tremor in her voice, or a flash of the eye, which
indicated that which, under the supervision of
the usually astute dowager her mother, she dared
scarcely to betray—an interest in one such as me
—it would prove at least that my presence was
not indifferent to her. Thus much only did I
hope, and of such faint hope had my heart been
full until now, when I heard all this; and if I
was piqued by her absence, I was still more by
the cause of it; though had I reflected for a
moment, I ought to have known that the very
circumstances under which I had last parted from
her in London, with an expected avowal all but
uttered and hovering on my lips when leading her
to the carriage, were sufficient to preclude a girl
so proud as she from coming to meet me, even in
the avenue, and when accompanied by Winifred
and Dora Lloyd.

'Is Mr. Guilfoyle a musician?' I asked.

'A little,' replied Dora; 'plays and sings too;
but I can't help laughing at him—and it is so
rude.'

'He says that he is a friend of yours, Harry

Hardinge; is he so?' asked Sir Madoc, with his bushy brows depressed for a moment.

'Well, if losing to him once at pool mysteriously, also on a certain horse, while he scratched out of its engagements another on which I stood sure to win, make a friend, he is one. I have met him at his club, and should think that he—he—'

'Is not a good style of fellow, in fact,' said Sir Madoc in a low tone, and rather bluntly.

'Perhaps so; nor one I should like to see at Craigaderyn Court.' I cared not to add 'especially in the society of Lady Cressingham,' after whom he dangled, on the strength of some attentions or friendly services performed on the Continent.

'And so you lost money to him? We have a Welsh proverb beginning, *Dyled ar bawb*—'

'We shall have barely time to dress, dear papa,' said Miss Lloyd, increasing the speed of her horse, as she seemed to dread the Welsh proclivities of her parent; 'and remember that we have quite a dinner-party to-day.'

'Yes,' added Dora; 'two country M.P.s are coming; but, O dear! they will talk nothing but blue-book with papa, or about the crops, fat pigs, and the county pack; and shake their heads about ministerial policy and our foreign prestige, whatever that may be. Then we have an Indian colonel with only half a liver, the doctor says, and two Indian judges without any at all.'

'Dora!' exclaimed Miss Lloyd in a tone of expostulation.

'Well, it is what the doctor said,' persisted Dora; 'and if he is wrong can I help it?'

'But people don't talk of such things.'

'Then people shouldn't have them.'

'A wild Welsh girl this,' said Sir Madoc; 'neither schooling in Switzerland nor London has tamed her.'

'And we are to have several county gentlemen who are great in the matters of turnips, top-dressing, and Welsh mutton; four young ladies, each with a flirtation on hand; and four old ones, deep in religion and scandal, flannel and coals for the poor; so, Mr. Hardinge, you and Mr. Caradoc will be quite a double relief to us—to me, certainly.'

'O, Dora, how your tongue runs on!' exclaimed Winifred.

'And then we have Lady Naseby to act as

materfamilias, and play propriety for us all in black velvet and diamonds. Winny, eldest daughter of the house, is evidently unequal to the task.'

'And the coming fête,' said I, ' is it in honour of anything in particular ?'

'Yes, something very particular indeed,' replied Dora.

' Of what ?'

' Me.'

' You !'

' My birthday—I shall be eighteen,' she added, shaking back the heavy masses of her golden hair.

'And she has actually promised to have one round dance with Lord Pottersleigh,' said Winny, laughing heartily.

'I did but promise out of mischief; I trust, however, the Viscount will leave off his goloshes for that day, though we are to dance on the grass, or I hope he may forget all about it. Old Potter, I call him,' added the young lady in a *sotto-voce* to me, ' at least, when the Cressinghams are not present.'

' Why them especially ?'

' Because he is such a particular friend of theirs.'

This was annoyance number two; for this wealthy but senile old peer had been a perpetual adorer of Lady Estelle, favoured too, apparently, by her mother, and had been on more than one occasion a *bête noire* to me; and now I was to meet him here again!

'Papa has told you that I mean to part with my poor pet goat—Carneydd Llewellyn, so called from the mountain whence he came. He is to be sent to the regiment—in your care, too.'

'Why deprive yourself of a favourite? Why deprive it of such care as yours? Among soldiers,' said I, 'the poor animal will sorely miss the kindness and caresses you bestow upon it.'

'I shall be so pleased to think that our Welsh Fusileers, in the lands to which they are going, will have something so characteristic to remind them of home, of the wild hills of Wales, perhaps to make them think of the donor. Besides, papa says the corps has never been without this emblem of the old Principality since it was raised in the year of the Revolution.'

'Most true; but how shall I—how shall *we* —ever thank you?'

I could see that her nether lip—a lovely little

pouting lip it was—quivered slightly, and that
her eyes were full of strange light, though bent
downward on her horse's mane; and now I felt
that, for reasons apparent enough, I was cold, even
unkind, to this warm-hearted girl; for we had
been better and dearer friends before we knew the
Cressinghams.

She checked her horse a little abruptly, and
began to address some of the merest commonplaces to Phil Caradoc; who, with his thick brown
curly hair parted in the middle, his smiling handsome face and white regular teeth, was finding
great favour in the eyes of the laughing Dora.
But now we were drawing near Craigaderyn
Court.

The scenery was Welsh, and yet the house and
all its surroundings were in character genuinely
English, though to have hinted so much might
have piqued Sir Madoc. The elegance and com-
fort of the mansion were English, and English too
was the rich verdure of the velvet lawn and the
stately old chase, the trees of which were ancient
enough—some of them at least—to have shel-
tered Owen Glendower, or echoed to the bugle of
Llewellyn ap Seisalt, whose tall grave-stone

stands amid the battle-mounds on grassy Castell Coch.

At a carved and massive entrance-door we alighted, assisted the ladies to dismount, and then, gathering up their trains, they swept merrily up the steps and into the house, to prepare for dinner; while Sir Madoc, ere he permitted us to retire, though the first bell had been rung, led us into the hall; a low-ceiled, irregular, and oak-panelled room, decorated with deers' antlers, foxes' brushes crossed, and stuffed birds of various kinds, among others a gigantic golden eagle shot by himself on Snowdon. This long apartment was so cool that, though the season was summer, a fire burned in the old stone fireplace; and on a thick rug before it lay a great, rough, red-eyed staghound, that made one think of the faithful brach that saved Llewellyn's heir.

The windows were half shaded by scarlet hangings; a hunting-piece or two by Sneyders, with pictures of departed favourites, horses and dogs, indicated the tastes of the master of the house and of his ancestors; and there too was the skull of the *last* wolf killed in Wales, more than a century ago, grinning on an oak bracket.

The butler, Owen Gwyllim, who occasionally officiated as a harper, especially at Yule, was speedily in attendance, and Sir Madoc insisted on our joining him in a stiff glass of brandy-and-water, ' as a whet,' he said ; and prior to tossing off which he gave a hoarse guttural toast in Welsh, which his butler alone understood, and at which he laughed heartily, with the indulged familiarity of an old servant.

I then retired to make an unusually careful toilette ; to leave nothing undone or omitted in the way of cuffs, studs, rings, and so forth, in all the minor details of masculine finery; hearing the while from a distance the notes of a piano in another wing of the house come floating through an open window. The air was German ;—could I doubt whose white fingers were gliding over the keys, and *who* might be standing by, and feeling himself, perhaps, somewhat master of the situation ?

CHAPTER V.

CRAIGADERYN COURT.

APART from Welsh fable and tradition, the lands of Craigaderyn had been in possession of Sir Madoc's family for many ages, and for more generations of the line of Lloyd; but the mansion, the Court itself, is not older than the Stuart times, and portions of it were much more recent, particularly the library, the shelves of which were replete with all that a gentleman's library should contain; the billiard-room and gun-room, where all manner of firearms, from the old long-barrelled fowling-piece of Anne's time down to Joe Manton and Colt's revolver, stood side by side on racks; the kennels, where many a puppy yelped; and the stable-court, where hoofs rang and stall-collars jangled, and where Mr. Bob Spurrit—a long-bodied, short-and-crooked-legged specimen of the Welsh groom—reigned supreme, and watered and

corned his nags by the notes of an ancient clock
in the central tower—a clock said to have been
brought as spoil from the church of Todtenhausen,
by Sir Madoc's grandfather, after he led the Welsh
Fusileers at the battle of Minden.

Masses of that 'rare old plant, the ivy green,'
heavy, leafy, and overlapping each other, shrouded
great portions of the house. Oriels, full of small
panes and quaint coats of arms, abutted here and
there; while pinnacles and turrets, vanes, and
groups of twisted, fluted, or garlanded stone
chimney stacks, rose sharply up to break the sky-
line. And many a panel and scutcheon of stone
were there, charged with the bend, ermine, and
pean of Lloyd—the lion rampant wreathed with
oak, and armed with a sword—and the heraldic
cognizance of many a successive matrimonial alli-
ance.

Some portions of the house, where the walls
were strong and the lower story vaulted, were
associated, of course, with visits from Llewellyn
and Owen Glendower; and there also abode—
a ghost. The park, too, was not without its old
memories and traditions. Many of its trees were
descendants of an ancient grove dedicated to

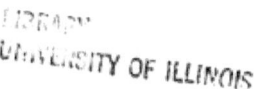

Druidic worship; and bones frequently found there were alleged by some to be the relics of human sacrifice, by others to be those of Roman or of Saxon warriors slain by the sturdy Britons who, under Cadwallader, Llewellyn of the Torques, or some other hero of the Pendragonate, had held, in defiance of both, the *caer* or fort on the summit of Craigaderyn. But the woodlands on which Sir Madoc most prided himself were those of the old acorn season, when Nature planted her own wild forests, and sowed the lawn out of her own lawns, as some writer has it. They were unquestionably the most picturesque, but the trim and orderly chase was not without its beauties too, and there had many grand Eisteddfoddiau been held under the auspices of Sir Madoc, and often fifty harpers at a time had made the woods ring to ' The noble Race of Shenkin,' or ' The March of the Men of Harlech.'

The old Court and its surroundings were such as to make one agree with what Lord Lyttelton wrote of another Welsh valley, where 'the mountains seemed placed to guard the charming retreat from invasions ; and where, with the woman one loves, the friend of one's heart, and a good library, one might pass an age, and think it a day.'

The ghost was a tall thin figure, dressed some-what in the costume of Henry VIII.'s time; but his full-skirted doublet with large sleeves, the cap bordered with ostrich feathers, the close tight hose, and square-toed shoes, were all deep black; hence his, or *its*, aspect was sombre in the extreme, shadowy and uncertain too, as he was only visible in the twilight of eve, or the first dim and similarly uncertain light of the early dawn; and these alleged appearances have been chiefly on St. David's day, the 1st of March, and were preceded by the sound of a harp about the place—but a harp *unseen*.

He was generally supposed to leave, or be seen quitting, a portion of the house, where the old wall was shrouded with ivy, and to walk or glide swiftly and steadily, without casting either shadow or foot-mark on the grass, towards a certain ancient tree in the park, where he disappeared—faded, or melted out of sight. On the wall beneath the ivy being examined, a door—the portion of an earlier structure—was discovered to have been built up, but none knew when or why; and tradition averred that those who had seen him pass—for none dared follow—towards the old tree, could make out that his figure and face were those of a man in the prime of life, but the expression of the latter was sad, solemn, resolute, and gloomy.

The origin of the legend, as told to me by Winifred Lloyd, referred to a period rather remote in history, and was to the following effect.

Some fifteen miles southward from Craigaderyn is a quaint and singular village named Dinas Mowddwy, situated very strangely on the shelf of a steep mountain overlooking the Dyfi stream—a lofty spot commanding a view of the three beautiful valleys of the Ceryst; but this place was in past times the abode and fortress of a peculiar and terrible tribe, called the Gwylliad Cochion, or Red-haired Robbers, who made all North Wales, but more particularly their own district, a byeword and reproach, from the great extent and savage nature of the outrages they committed by fire and sword; so that to this day, we are told, there may be seen, in some of the remote mountain hamlets, more especially in Cemmaes near the sea, the well-sharpened scythe-blades, which were placed in the chimney-corners overnight, to be ready for them in case of a sudden attack. They were great crossbowmen, those out-

laws, and never failed in their aim; and so, like
the broken clans upon the Highland border, they
levied black mail on all, till the night of the 1st of
March 1534; when, during a terrific storm of
thunder, lightning, and wind, Sir Jorwerth Lloyd
of Craigaderyn, John Wynne ap Meredydd, and a
baron named Owen, scaled the mountain at the
head of their followers, fell on them sword in
hand, and after slaying a great number, hung one
hundred of them in a row.

One wretched mother, a red-haired Celt, begged
hard and piteously to have her youngest son
spared; but Sir Jorwerth was relentless, so the
young robber perished with the rest. Then the
woman rent her garments, and laying bare her
bosom, said it had nursed other sons and daughters, who would yet wash their hands in the blood
of them all. Owen was waylaid and slain by them
at a place named to this day Llidiart-y-Barwn, or
the Baron's Gate, and Meredydd fell soon after;
but for Lloyd the woman, who was a reputed
witch, had prepared another fate, as if aiming at
the destruction of his soul as well as his body;
for after his marriage with Gwerfyl Owen, he fell
madly in love with a golden-haired girl whom he

met when hunting in the forest near Craigaderyn; and as he immediately relinquished all attendance at church and all forms of prayer, and seemed to be besotted by her, the girl was averred to be an evil spirit, as she was never seen save in his company, and then only (by those who watched and lurked) 'in the glimpses of the moon.'

On the third St. David's eve after the slaughter at Dinas Mowddwy, he was seated with Gwerfyl in her chamber, listening to a terrific storm of wind and rain that swept through the valley, overturning the oldest trees, and shaking the walls of the ancient house, while the lightning played about the dim summits of Snowdon, and every mountain stream and *rhaidr*, or cataract, rolled in foam and flood to Llyn Alwen or the Conway.

On a tabourette near his knee she sat, lovingly clasping his hand between her own two, for he seemed restless, petulant, and gloomy, and had his cloak and cap at hand, as if about to go forth, though the weather was frightful.

'Jorwerth,' said she softly, 'the last time there was such a storm as this was on that terrible night—you remember?'

'When we cut off the Gwylliad Cochion—yes,

root and branch, sparing, as we thought, none, while the rain ran through my armour as through a waterspout.   But why speak of it, to-night especially? Yes, root and branch, even while that woman vowed vengeance,' he added, grinding his teeth.   'But what sound is that?'

'Music,' she replied, rising and looking round with surprise; but his tremulous hand, and, more than that, the sudden pallor of his face, arrested her, while the strains of a small harp, struck wildly and plaintively, came at times between the fierce gusts of wind that shook the forest trees and the hiss of the rain on the window-panes without.   Louder they seemed to come, and to be more emphatic and sharp; and, as he heard them, a violent trembling and cold perspiration came over all the form of Sir Jorwerth Lloyd.

'Heaven pity the harper who is abroad to-night!' said Gwerfyl, clasping her white hands.

'Let Hell do so, rather!' was the fierce response of her husband, as his eyes filled with a strange light.

At that moment a hand knocked on the window, and the startled wife, as she crouched by her husband's side, could see that it was small and delicate, wondrously beautiful too, and radiant with gems or glittering raindrops; and now her husband trembled more violently than ever.

Gwerfyl crossed herself, and rushed to the window.

'Strange,' said she; 'I can see no one.'

'No one in human form, perhaps,' replied her husband gloomily, as he lifted his cloak. 'Look again, dear wife.'

The lady did so, and fancied that close to the window-pane she could see a female face—anon she could perceive that it was small and beautiful, with hair of golden red, all wavy, and, strange to say, unwetted by the rain, and with eyes that were also of golden red, but with a devilish smile and glare and glitter in them and over all her features, as they appeared, but to vanish, as the successive flashes of lightning passed. With terror and foreboding of evil, she turned to her startled husband. He was a pale and handsome man, with an aquiline nose, a finely-cut mouth and chin; but now his lips were firmly compressed, a flashing and fiery light seemed to sparkle in his eyes, his forehead was covered with lines, and the veins of his temples were swollen, while his black hair and moustache seemed to have actually become streaked with gray. What unknown emotion caused all this ? There were power and passion in his bearing ; but something strange, and dark, and demon-like was brooding in his soul. The white drops glittered on his brow as he threw his cloak about him, and *then* the notes of the harp were heard, as if struck triumphantly and joyously.

'Stay, stay ! leave me not !' implored his wife on her knees, in a sudden access of terror and pity, that proved greater even than love.

'I cannot—I cannot ! God pardon me and bless you, dear, dear wife, but go I must !'

('Exactly like Rudolph, as we saw him last night in the opera, breaking away from his followers when he heard the voice of Lurline singing amid the waters of the Rhine,' added Winifred in a parenthesis, as she laid her hand timidly on my arm.)

She strove on her knees to place in his hand the small ivory-bound volume of prayers which ladies then carried slung by a chain at their girdle, even as a watch is now ; but he thrust it aside, as if it scorched his fingers. Then he kissed her wildly, and broke away.

She sprang from the floor, but he was gone—gone swiftly into the forest; and with sorrow and prayer in her heart his wife stealthily followed him.

By this time the sudden storm had as suddenly ceased; already the gusty wind had died away, and no trace of it remained, save the strewn leaves and a quivering in the dripping branches; the white clouds were sailing through the blue sky, and whiter still, in silvery sheen the moonlight fell aslant in patches through the branches on the glittering grass.

Amid that sheen she saw the dark figure of her husband passing, gliding onward to the old oak tree, and Gwerfyl shrunk behind another, as the notes of the infernal harp—for such she judged it to be—fell upon her ear.

'You have come, my beloved,' said a sweet voice; and she saw the same strangely-beautiful girl with the red-golden hair, her skin of wondrous whiteness, and eyes that glittered with devilish triumph, though to Jorwerth Du they seemed only filled with ardour and the light of passionate love, even as the beauty of her form seemed all round and white and perfect; but lo! to the eyes of his

wife, who was under *no spell*, that form was fast
becoming like features in a dissolving view, changed
to that of extreme old age—gray hairs and wrin-
kles seemed to come with every respiration; for
this mysterious love, who had bewitched her husband, was some evil spirit or demon of the
woods.

'How long you have been!' said she reproachfully, for even the sweetness of her tone had
suddenly passed away; 'so long that already age
seems to have come upon me.'

'Pardon me; have I not sworn to love you for
ever and ever, though neither of us is immortal?'

'You are ready?' said she, laying her head
on his breast.

'Yes, my own wild love!'

'Then let us go.'

All beauty of form had completely passed away,
and now Gwerfyl saw her handsome husband in
the arms of a very hag; hollow-cheeked, toothless,
almost fleshless, with restless shifty eyes, and
gray elf-locks like the serpents of Medusa; a hag
beyond all description hideous: and her long,
lean, shrivelled arms she wound lovingly and triumphantly around him. Her eyes gleamed like

two live coals as he kissed her wildly and passionately from time to time, the full blaze of the moonlight streaming upon both their forms.

Gwerfyl strove to pray, to cry aloud, to move. But her tongue refused its office, and her lips were powerless; all capability of volition had left her, and she was as it were rooted to the spot. A moment more, and a dark cloud came over the moon, causing a deeper shadow under the old oak tree.

Then a shriek escaped her, and when again the moon shone forth on the green grass and the gnarled tree, Gwerfyl alone was there—her husband and the hag had disappeared. Neither was ever seen more.

North Wales is the most primitive portion of the country, and it is there that such fancies and memories still linger longest; and such was the little family legend told me by Winifred Lloyd. I was thinking over it now, recalling the earnest expression of her bright soft face and intelligent eyes, and the tone of her pleasantly modulated voice, when she, half laughingly and half seriously, had related it, with more point than I can give it, while we sat in a corner and somewhat apart from

every one—on the first night I met the Cressinghams—in a crowded London ballroom, amid the
heat, the buzz, and crush of the season—about
the last place in the world to hear a story of
diablerie; and 'the old time' seemed to come
again, as I descended to the drawing-room, to
meet her and Lady Estelle.

CHAPTER VI.

THREE GRACES.

ALREADY having met and been welcomed by my host and his daughters, my first glances round the room were in search of Lady Estelle and her mother. About eighteen persons were present, mostly gentlemen, and I instinctively made my way to where she I sought was seated, idling over a book of prints. Two or three gentlemen were exclusively in conversation with her; Sir Madoc, who was now in evening costume, for one.

'Come, Harry,' said he, 'here is a fair friend to whom I wish to present you.'

'You forget, Sir Madoc, that I said we had met before; Mr. Hardinge and I are almost old friends —the friends of a season, at least,' said Lady Estelle, presenting her hand to me with a bright but calm and decidedly conventional smile, and with the most perfect self-possession.

'It makes me so very happy to meet you again,' said I in a low voice, the tone of which she could not mistake.

'Mamma, too, will be *so* delighted—you were quite a favourite with her.'

I bowed, as if accepting for fact a sentiment of which I was extremely doubtful, and then after a little pause she added,.

'Mamma always preferred your escort, you remember.'

Of that I was aware, when she wished to leave some more eligible *parti*—old Lord Pottersleigh, for instance—to take charge of her daughter.

'I am so pleased that we are to see a little more of you, ere you depart for the East; whence, I hear, you are bound,' said she after a little pause.

Simple though the words, they made my heart beat happily, and I dreaded that some sharp observer might read in my eyes the expression which I knew could not be concealed from her; and now I turned to look for some assistance from Winifred Lloyd; but, though observing us, she was apparently busy with Caradoc; luckily for me, perhaps, as there was something of awkwardness in my

position with her.   I had flirted rather too much
at one time with Winny—been almost tender—but
nothing more.   Now I loved Lady Estelle, and
that love was indeed destitute of all ambition,
though the known difficulties attendant on the
winning of such a hand as hers, added zest and
keenness to its course.

When I looked at Winifred and saw how fair
and attractive she was, 'a creature so compact
and complete,' as Caradoc phrased it, with such
brilliance of complexion, such deep violet eyes
and thick dark wavy hair; and when I thought of
the girl's actual wealth, and her kind old father's
great regard for me, it seemed indeed that I might
do well in offering my heart where there was little
doubt it would be accepted; but the more stately
and statuesque beauty, the infinitely greater personal attractions of Lady Estelle dazzled me, and
rendered me blind to Winny's genuine goodness
of soul.

The latter was every way a most attractive
girl. Dora was quite as much so, in her own droll
and jolly way; but Lady Estelle possessed that
higher style of loveliness and bearing so difficult
to define; and though less natural perhaps than

the Lloyds, she had usually that calm, placid, and unruffled or settled expression of features so pecu- liar to many Englishwomen of rank and culture, yet they could light up at times; then, indeed, she became radiant; and now, in full dinner dress, she seemed to look pretty much as I had seemed to see her in that haughty full-length by the President of the R. A., with an admiring and critical crowd about it.

The three girls I have named were all hand- some—each sufficiently so to have been the belle of any room; yet, though each was different in type from the other, they were all thoroughly English; perhaps Sir Madoc would have reminded me that two were Welsh. The beauty of Winifred and Dora was less regular; yet, like Lady Estelle, in their faces each feature seemed so charmingly suited to the rest, and all so perfect, that I doubt much the story that Canova had sixty models for his single Venus, or that Zeuxis of Heraclea had even five for his Helen.

Lady Estelle Cressingham was tall and full in form, with a neck that rose from her white shoulders like that of some perfect Greek model; her smile, when real, was very captivating; her eyes were dark and deep, and softly lidded with long lashes; they had neither the inquiring nor soft pleading expression of Winifred's, nor the saucy drollery of Dora's, yet at times they seemed to have the power of both; for they were eloquent eyes, and, as a writer has it, ' could light up her whole *personnel* as if her whole body thought.'

Her colour was pale, almost creamy; her features clearly cut and delicate. She had a well-curved mouth, a short upper lip and chin, that indicated what she did not quite possess—decision. Her thick hair, which in its darkness contrasted so powerfully with her paleness, came somewhat well down, in what is called ' a widow's peak,' on a forehead that was broad rather than low. Her taste was perfect in dress and jewelry; for though but a girl in years, she had been carefully trained, and knew nearly as much of the world—at least of *the* exclusive world in which she lived—as her cold and unimpressionable mamma, who seemed to be but a larger, fuller, older, and more stately version of herself; certainly much more of that selfish world than I, a line subaltern of seven years' foreign service, could know.

A few words more, concerning my approaching departure for the East, were all that could pass between us then; for the conversation was, of course, general, and of that enforced and heavy nature which usually precedes a dinner-party; but our memories and our thoughts were nevertheless our own still, as I could see when her glance met mine occasionally.

War was new to Britain then, and thus, even in the society at Craigaderyn Court, Caradoc and I, as officers whose regiment had already departed —more than all, as two of the Royal Welsh Fusileers—found ourselves rather objects of interest, and at a high premium.

'Ah, the dooce! Hardinge, how d'you do, how d'you do? Not off to the seat of war' (he pronounced it *waw*), 'to tread the path of glory that leads to—where *does* old Gray say it leads to?' said a thin wiry-looking man of more than middle height and less than middle age, his well-saved hair carefully parted in the centre, a glass in his eye, and an easy *insouciance* that bordered on insolence in his tone and bearing, as he came bluntly forward, and interrupted me while paying the necessary court to 'Mamma Cressingham,' who received me with simple politeness, nothing more.

I could not detect the slightest cordiality in her tone or eye. Though in the *Army List*, my name was unchronicled by Debrett, and might never be.

I bowed to the speaker, who was the identical Mr. Hawkesby Guilfoyle of whom I have already spoken, and with whom I felt nettled for presuming to place himself on such a footing of apparent familiarity with me, from the simple circumstance that I had more than once — I scarcely knew how—lost money to him.

'I am going Eastward ere long, at all events,' said I; 'and I cannot help thinking that some of you many idlers here could not do better than take a turn of service against the Russians too.'

'It don't pay, my dear fellow; moreover, I prefer to be one of the gentlemen of England, who live at home at ease. I shall be quite satisfied with reading all about it, and rejoicing in your exploits.'

I smiled and bowed, but felt that he was closely scrutinising me through his glass, which he held in its place by a muscular contraction of the left eye; and I felt moreover, instinctively and intuitively, by some magnetic influence, that this man was my enemy, and yet I had done him

no wrong. The aversion was certainly mutual.
It was somewhat of the impulse that led Tom
Brown of old to dislike Dr. Fell, yet, in my in-
stance, it was not exactly without knowing ' why.'

I had quickly read the character of this Mr.
Guilfoyle. He had cold, cunning, and shifty eyes
of a greenish yellow colour. They seldom smiled,
even when his mouth did, if that can be called a
smile which is merely a grin from the teeth out-
wards. He was undoubtedly gentlemanlike in air
and appearance, always correct in costume, suave
to servility when it suited his purpose, but
daringly insolent when he could venture to be so
with impunity. He had that narrowness of mind
which made him counterfeit regret for the disaster
of his best friend, while secretly exulting in it, if
that friend could serve his purposes no more ; the
praise or success of another never failed to excite
either his envy or his malice ; and doating on
himself, he thought that all who knew him should
quarrel with those against whom he conceived
either spleen or enmity.

A member of a good club in town, he was
fashionable, moderately dissipated, and rather
handsome in person. No one knew exactly from

what source his income was derived; but vague hints of India stock, foreign bonds, and so forth, served to satisfy the few—and in the world of London few they were indeed—who cared a jot about the matter.

Such was Mr. Hawkesby Guilfoyle, of whom the reader shall hear more in these pages.

'And so you don't approve of risking your valuable person in the service of the country?' said I, in a tone which I felt to be a sneering one.

'No; I am disposed to be rather economical of it—think myself too good-looking, perhaps, to fill a hole in a trench. Ha, ha! Moreover, what the deuce do I want with glory or honour?' said he in a lower tone; 'are not self-love or interest, rather than virtue, the true motives of most of our actions?'

'Do you think so?'

'Yes, by Jove! I do.'

'A horrid idea, surely!'

'Not at all. Besides, virtues, as they are often called, are too often only vices disguised.'

'The deuce!' said Caradoc, who overheard us; 'I don't understand this paradox.'

'Nor did I intend *you* to do so,' replied the

other, in a tone that, to say the least of it, was offensive, and made Phil's eyes sparkle. 'But whether in pursuit of vice or virtue, it is an awkward thing when the ruling passion makes one take a wrong turn in life.'

'The ruling passion?' said I, thinking of the money I had lost to him.

'Yes, whether it be ambition, avarice, wine, or love,' he replied, his eyes going involuntarily towards Lady Estelle; 'but at all times there is nothing like taking precious good care of number one; and so, were I a king, I should certainly reign for myself.'

'And be left to yourself,' said I, almost amused by this avowed cynicism and selfishness.

'Well, as Prince Esterhazy said, when he did me the honour to present me with this ring,' he began, playing the while with a splended brilliant, which sparkled on one of his fingers.

But what the Prince had said I was never fated to know; for the aphorisms of Mr. Guilfoyle were cut short by the welcome sound of the dinner-gong, and in file we proceeded through the corridor and hall to the dining-room, duly mar-shalled between two rows of tall liverymen in powder and plush, Sir Madoc leading the way with the Countess on his arm, her long sweeping skirt so stiff with brocade, that, as Caradoc whispered, it looked like our regimental colours.

Lady Estelle was committed to the care of a stout old gentleman, who was the exact counterpart of our host, and whose conversation, as it evidently failed to amuse, bored her. Miss Lloyd was led by Caradoc, and Dora fell to my care. Of the other ladies I took little heed; neither did I much of the sumptuous dinner, which passed away as other dinners do, through all its courses, with entrées and relays of various wines, the serving up of the latter proving in one sense a nuisance, from the absurd breaks caused thereby in the conversation.

The buzz of voices was pretty loud at times, for many of the guests were country gentlemen, hale and hearty old fellows some of them, who laughed with right good will, not caring whether to do so was good *ton* or not. But while listening to the lively prattle of Dora Lloyd, I could not refrain from glancing ever and anon to where Estelle Cressingham, looking so radiant, yet withal 'so delicately white' in her complexion,

her slender throat and dazzling shoulders, her
thick dark hair and tiny ears, at which the diamond pendants sparkled, sat listening to her
elderly bore, smiling assents from time to time
out of pure complaisance, and toying with her
fruit knife when the dessert came, her hands and
arms seeming so perfect in form and colour, and
on more than one occasion—when her mamma
was engrossed by courteous old Sir Madoc, who
could 'talk peerage,' and knew the quartering of
arms better than the Garter King or Rouge
Dragon—giving me a bright intelligent smile,
that made my heart beat happily; all the more
so that I had been afflicted by some painful sus-
picion of coldness in her first reception of me—
a coldness rather deduced from her perfect self-
possession—while I had been farther annoyed to
find that her somewhat questionable admirer,
Guilfoyle, was seated by her side, with a lady
whose presence he almost ignored in his desire to
be pleasing elsewhere.

Yet, had it been otherwise, if anything might
console a man for fancied coldness in the woman
he loved, or for a partial separation from her by a
few yards of mahogany, it should be the lively

rattle of a lovely girl of eighteen; but while listening and replying to Dora, my thoughts and wishes were with another.

'I told you how it would be, Mr. Hardinge,' whispered Dora; 'that the staple conversation of the gentlemen, if it didn't run on the county pack, would be about horses and cattle, sheep, horned and South Down; or on the British Constitution, which must be a very patched invention, to judge by all they say of it.'

I confessed inwardly that much of what went on around me was so provincial and local—the bishop's visitation, the parish poor, crops and game, grouse and turnips—and proved such boredom, that, but for the smiling girl beside me, with her waggish eyes and pretty ways, and the longing and hope to have more of the society of Lady Estelle, I could have wished myself back at the mess of the dépôt battalion in Winchester. Yet this restlessness was ungrateful; for Craigaderyn was as much a home to me as if I had been a son of the house, and times there were when the girls, like their father, called me simply 'Harry,' by my Christian name.

The long and stately dining-room, like other

parts of the house, was well hung with portraits. At one end was a full-length of Sir Madoc in his scarlet coat and yellow-topped boots, seated on his favourite bay mare 'Irish Jumper,' with mane and reins in hand, a brass horn slung over his shoulder, and looking every inch like what he was— the M.F.H. of the county, trotting to cover. Opposite, of course, was his lady—it might almost have passed for a likeness of Winifred—done several years ago, her dress of puce velvet cut low to show her beautiful outline, but otherwise very full indeed, as she leaned in the approved fashion against a vase full of impossible flowers beside a column and draped curtain, in what seemed a windy and draughty staircase, a view of Snowdon in the distance. 'Breed and blood,' as Sir Madoc used to say, 'in every line of her portrait, from the bridge of her nose to the heel of her slipper;' for she was a lineal descendant of *y Marchog gwyllt o' Cae Hywel*, or 'the wild Knight of Caehowel,' a circumstance he valued more than all her personal merits and goodness of heart.

Some of Dora's remarks about the family portraits elicited an occasional glance of reprehension from the Dowager of Naseby, who thought such relics or evidences of descent were not to be treated lightly.

On my inquiring who that lady in the very low dress with the somewhat dishevelled hair was, I had for answer, 'A great favourite of Charles II., Mr. Hardinge—an ancestress of ours. Papa knows her name. There was some lively scandal about her, of course. And that is her brother beside her—he in the rose-coloured doublet and black wig. He was killed in a duel about a young lady—run clean through the heart by one of the Wynnes of Llanrhaidr, at the Ring in Hyde Park.'

'When men risked their lives so, love must have been very earnest in those days,' said Lady Estelle.

'And very fearful,' said the gentler Winny. 'It is said the lady's name was engraved on the blade of the sword that slew him.'

'A duel! How delightful to be the heroine of a duel!' exclaimed the volatile Dora.

'And who is that pretty woman in the sacque and puffed cap?' asked Caradoc, pointing to a brisk-looking dame in a long stomacher. She was well rouged, rather *décolletée*, had a roguish kissing-patch in the corner of her mouth, and looked very like Dora indeed.

'Papa's grandmother, who insisted on wearing a white rose when she was presented to the Elector at St. James's,' replied Dora; 'and her marriage to the heir of Craigaderyn is chronicled in the fashion of the Georgian era, by gossipping Mr. Sylvanus Urban, as that of "Mistress Betty Temple, an agreeable and modest young lady with 50,000l. fortune, from the eastward of Temple Bar." I don't think people were such tuft-hunters in those days as they are now. Do *you* think so, Mr. Guilfoyle? O, I am sure, that if all we read in novels is true, there must have been more romantic marriages and much more honest love long ago than we find in society now. What do you say to this, Estelle?'

But the fair Estelle only fanned herself, and replied by a languid smile, that somehow eluded when it might have fallen on *me*.

So while we lingered over the dessert (the pine-apples, peaches, grapes, and so forth being all the produce of Sir Madoc's own hot-houses), Dora resumed:

'And so, poor Harry Hardinge, in a few

weeks more you will be far away from us, and face to face with those odious Russians — in a real battle, perhaps. It is something terrible to think of! Ah, heavens, if you should be killed!' she added, as her smile certainly passed away for a moment.

'I don't think somehow there is very much danger of that—at least I can but hope—'

'Or wounded! If you should lose a leg— two legs perhaps—'

'He could scarcely lose *more*,' said Mr. Guil-foyle.

'And come home with wooden ones!' she continued, lowering her voice. 'You will look so funny! O, I could never love or marry a man with wooden stumps!'

'But,' said I, a little irritated that she should see anything so very amusing in this supposed contingency, 'I don't mean to marry *you*.'

'Of course not—I know that. It is Winny, papa thinks—or is it Estelle Cressingham you prefer?'

Lowly and whispered though the heedless girl said this, it reached the ears of Lady Estelle, and caused her to grow if possible paler, while I felt

my face suffused with scarlet; but luckily all now
rose from the table, as the ladies, led by Winifred,
filed back alone to the drawing-room; and I felt
that Dora's too palpable hints must have done
much to make or mar my cause—perhaps to gain
me the enmity of both her sister and the Lady
Estelle.

Sir Madoc assumed his daughter's place at the
head of the table, and beckoned *me* to take his
chair at the foot. Owen Gwyllim replenished the
various decanters and the two great silver jugs of
claret and burgundy, and the flow of conversation
became a little louder in tone, and of course less
reserved. I listened now with less patience to all
that passed around me, in my anxiety to follow
the ladies to the drawing-room. Every moment
spent out of *her* presence seemed doubly long and
doubly lost.

The chances of the coming war—*where* our
troops were to land, whether at Eupatoria or Pere-
cop, or were to await an attack where they were
literally rotting in the camp upon the Bulgarian
shore; their prospects of success, the proposed
bombardment of Cronstadt, the bewildering orders
issued to our admirals, the inane weakness and

pitiful vacillation, if not worse, of Lord Aberdeen's government, our total want of all preparation in the ambulance and commissariat services, even to the lack of sufficient shot, shell, and gunpowder—were all freely descanted on, and attacked, explained, or defended according to the politics or the views of those present; and Guilfoyle—who, on the strength of having been attaché at the petty German court of Catzenelnbogen, affected a great knowledge of continental affairs—indulged in much 'tall talk' on the European situation, till once more the county pack and hunting became the chief topic, and then too he endeavoured, but perhaps vainly, to take the lead.

'You talk of fox-hunting, gentlemen,' said he, raising his voice after a preliminary cough, 'and some of the anecdotes you tell of wonderful leaps, mistakes, and runs, with the cunning displayed by reynard on various occasions, such as hiding in a pool up to the snout, feigning death—a notion old as the days of Olaus Magnus—throwing dogs off the scent by traversing a running stream, and so forth, are all remarkable enough; but give me a good buck-hunt, such as I have seen in Croatia! When travelling there among

the mountains that lie between Carlstadt and the
Adriatic, I had the good fortune to reside for a
few weeks with my kind friend Ladislaus Count
Mosvina, Grand Huntsman to the Emperor of
Austria, and captain of the German Guard of
Arzieres, and who takes his title from that wine-
growing district, the vintage of which is fully
equal to the finest burgundy. The season was
winter. The snow lay deep among the frightful
valleys and precipices of the Vellibitch range,
and an enormous *rehbock*, or roebuck, fully five
feet in height to the shoulder, with antlers of vast
size—five feet, if an inch, from tip to tip—driven
from the mountains by the storm and *la bora*, the
biting north-east wind, took shelter in a thicket
near the house. Several shots were fired; but
no one, not even *I*, could succeed in hitting him,
till at last he defiantly and coolly fed among the
sheep, in the yard of the Count's home farm,
where, by the use of his antlers, he severely
wounded and disabled all who attempted to dis-
lodge him. At last four of the Count's farmers or
foresters—some of those Croatian boors who are
liable to receive twenty-five blows of a cudgel
yearly if they fail to engraft at least twenty-five

fruit-trees—undertook to slay or capture the intruder. But though they were powerful, hardy, and brave men, this devil of a *rehbock*, by successive blows of its antlers, fractured the skulls of two and the thigh-bones of the others, smashing them like tobacco-pipes, and made an escape to the mountains. A combined hunt was now ordered by my friend Mosvina, and all the gentlemen and officers in the *generalat* or district commanded by him set off, mounted and in pursuit. There were nearly a thousand horsemen; but the cavalry there are small and weak. *I* was perhaps the best mounted man in the field. We pursued it for fully twenty-five miles, by rocky hills and almost pathless woods, by ravines and rivers. Many of our people fell. Some got staked, were pulled from their saddles by trees, or tumbled off by running foul of wild swine. Many missed their way, grew weary, got imbogged in the half-frozen marshes, and so forth, till at last only the Count and I with four dogs were on his track, and when on it, we leaped no less than four frozen cataracts, each at least a hundred feet in height —'pon honour they were. We had gone almost neck and neck for a time; but the Grand Hunts-

man's horse began to fail him now (for we had
come over terrible ground, most of it being up-
hill), and ultimately it fell dead lame. Then
whoop—tally-ho! I spurred onward alone. Just
as the furious giant was coming to bay in a narrow gorge, and, fastening on his flanks and neck,
the maddened dogs were tearing him down, their
red jaws steaming in the frosty air, the Count
came up on foot, breathless and thoroughly blown,
to have the honour of slaying this antlered mon-
arch of the Dinovian Alps. But I was too quick
for him. I had sprung from my horse, and with
my unsheathed *hanshar* or Croatian knife had
flung myself, fearlessly and regardless of all danger, upon the buck, eluding a last and desperate
butt made at me with his pointed horns. Another
moment saw my knife buried to the haft in his
throat, and a torrent of crimson blood flowing
upon the snow. Then I courteously tendered my
weapon by the hilt to the Count, who, in admiration of my adroitness, presented me with this
ring—a very fine brilliant, you may perceive—
which his grandfather had received from the Em-
press Maria Theresa, and the pure gold of which is
native, from the sand upon the banks of the Drave.'

And as he concluded his anecdote, which he related with considerable pomposity and perfect coolness, he twirled round his finger this remarkable ring, of which I was eventually to hear more from time to time.

'So, out of a thousand Croatian horsemen, *you* were the only one in at the death! It says little for their manhood,' said an old fox-hunter, as he filled his glass with burgundy, and pretty palpably winked to Sir Madoc, under cover of an épergne.

'This may all be true, Harry, or not—only, *entre nous,* I don't believe it is,' said Phil Caradoc aside to me; 'for who here knows anything of Croatia? He might as well talk to old Gwyllim the butler, or any chance medley Englishman, of the land of Memnon and the hieroglyphics. This fellow Guilfoyle beats Munchausen all to nothing; but did he not before tell something *else* about that ring?'

'I don't remember; but now, Phil, that you have seen her,' said I, in a tone of tolerably-affected carelessness, 'what do you think of *la belle* Cressingham?'

'She is very handsome, certainly,' replied Phil

in the same undertone, and luckily looking at his glass and not at me ; 'a splendid specimen of her class—a proud and by no means bashful beauty.'

'Most things in this world are prized just as they are difficult of attainment, or are scarce. I reckon beauty among these, and no woman holds it cheap,' said I, not knowing exactly what to think of Caradoc's criticism. 'There is Miss Lloyd, for instance—'

'Ah,' said he, with honest animation, 'she is a beauty too, but a gentle and retiring one— a girl that is all sweetness and genuine goodness of heart.'

'With some dairy-farms in the midland counties, eh ?'

'The graces of such a girl are always the most attractive. We men are so constituted that we are apt to decline admiration where it is loftily courted or seemingly expected—as I fear it is in the case of Lady Cressingham — and to bestow it on the gentle and retiring.'

I felt there was much truth in my friend's remarks, and yet they piqued me so, that I rather turned from him coldly for the remainder of the evening.

'Her mother is haughty, intensely ambitious, and looks forward to a title for her as high, if not higher, than that her father bore,' I heard Sir Madoc say to a neighbour who had been talking on the same subject—the beauty of Lady Estelle; 'the old lady is half Irish and half Welsh.'

'Rather a combustible compound, I should think,' added Guilfoyle, as, after coffee and curaçoa, we all rose to join the ladies in the drawing-room.

CHAPTER VII.

PIQUE.

THE moment I entered the drawing-room, where Winifred Lloyd had been doing her utmost to amuse her various guests till we came, and where undoubtedly the ladies' faces grew brighter when we appeared, I felt conscious that the remark of the hoidenish Dora had done me some little mischief. I could read this in the face of the haughty Estelle, together with her fear that *others* might have heard it; thus, instead of seating myself near her, as I wished and had fully intended, I remained rather aloof, and leaving her almost exclusively to the industrious Guilfoyle, divided my time between listening to Winifred, who, with Caradoc, proceeded to perform the duet he had sent her from the barracks, and endeavouring to make myself agreeable to the

Countess—a process rather, I am sorry to say, somewhat of a task to me.

Though her dark hair was considerably seamed with gray, her forehead was without a line, smooth and unwrinkled as that of a child —care, thought, reflection, or sorrow had never visited *her*. Wealth and rank, with a naturally aristocratic indolence and indifference of mind, had made the ways of life and of the world— at least, the world in which she lived—easy, soft, and pleasant, and all her years had glided brilliantly but monotonously on. She had married the late earl to please her family rather than herself, because he was undoubtedly an eligible *parti;* and she fully expected their only daughter to act exactly in the same docile manner. Her mien and air were stately, reserved, and uninviting; her eyes were cold, inquiring, and searching in expression, and I fancied that they seemed to watch and follow me, as if she really and naturally suspected me of 'views,' or, as she would have deemed them, *designs.*

Amid the commonplaces I was venturing to utter to this proud, cold, and decidedly unpleasant old dame, whose goodwill and favour I was sedulously anxious to gain, it was impossible for me to avoid hearing some remarks that Sir Madoc made concerning me, and to her daughter.

'I am so glad you like my young friend, Lady Estelle,' said the bluff baronet, leaning over her chair, his rubicund face beaming with smiles and happiness; for he was in best of moods after a pleasant dinner, with agreeable society and plenty of good wine.

'Who told you that I did so?' asked she, looking up with fresh annoyance, yet not un-mixed with drollery, in her beautiful face.

'Dora and Winny too; and I am so pleased, for he is an especial friend of ours. I love the lad for his dead mother's sake—she was an old flame of mine in my more romantic days—and doesn't he deserve it? What do you think the colonel of his old corps says of him?'

'Really, Sir Madoc, I know not—that he is quite a lady-killer, perhaps; to be such is the ambition of most young subalterns.'

'Better than that. He wrote me, that young Hardinge is all that a British officer ought to be; that he has a constitution of iron—could sleep out in all weathers, in a hammock or under a tree—till the fever attacked him at least. If provisions were scanty, he'd share his last biscuit with a comrade; on the longest and hottest march he never fell out or became knocked up; and more than once he has been seen carrying a couple of muskets, the arms of those whose strength had failed them. "I envy the Royal Welsh their acquisition, and regret that *we* have lost him"—these were the colonel's very words.'

Had I fee'd or begged him to plead my cause, he could not have been more earnest or emphatic.

'For heaven's sake, Sir Madoc, do stop this overpowering eulogium,' said I; 'it is impossible for one not to overhear, when one's own name is mentioned. But did the colonel really say all this of me?'

'All, and more, Harry.'

'It should win him a diploma of knight-bachelor,' said Lady Estelle, laughing, 'a C.B., perhaps a baronetcy.'

'Nay,' said Sir Madoc; 'such rewards are reserved now for toad-eaters, opulent traders, tuft-hunters, and ministerial tools; the days when true merit was rewarded are gone, my dear Lady Estelle.'

The duet over, Phil Caradoc drew near me, for evidently he was not making much progress with Miss Lloyd.

'Well, Phil,' said I in a low voice, 'among those present have you seen your ideal of woman?'

'Can't say,' said he rather curtly; 'but *you* have, at all events, old fellow, and I think Sir Madoc has done a good stroke of business for you by his quotation of the colonel's letter. I heard him all through our singing—the old gentleman has no idea of a *sotto-voce*, and talks always as if he were in the hunting-field. By Jove, Harry, you grow quite pink!' he continued, laughing. 'I see how the land lies with you; but as for "*la mère* Cressingham," she is an exclusive of the first water, a match-maker by reputation; and I fear you have not the ghost of a chance with her.'

'Hush, Caradoc,' said I, glancing nervously about me; 'remember that we are not at Winchester, or inside the main-guard, just now. But see, Lady Estelle and that fellow Guilfoyle are about to favour us,' I added, as the pale beauty spread her ample skirts over the piano-stool, with an air that, though all unstudied, seemed quite imperial, and ran her slender fingers rapidly over the white keys, preluding an air; while Guilfoyle, who had a tolerable voice and an intolerable amount of assurance, prepared to sing by fussily placing on the piano a piece of music, on the corner of which was written in a large and bold hand, evidently his own—'To Mr. H. Guilfoyle, from H.S.H. the Princess of Catzenelnbogen.'

'You must have been a special favourite with this lady,' said Estelle, ' as most of your German music is inscribed thus.'

'Yes, we were always exchanging our pieces and songs,' said he languidly and in a low voice close to her ear, yet not so low as to be unheard by me. 'I was somewhat of a favourite with her, certainly; but then the Princess was quite a privileged person.'

'In what respect?'

'She could flirt farther than any one, and yet never compromise herself. However, when she bestowed this ring upon me, on that day when I saved her life, by arresting her runaway horse on the very brink of the Rhine, I must own that his Highness the Prince was the reverse of pleased, and viewed me with coldness ever after; so that ultimately I resigned my office of attaché, just about the time I had the pleasure—may I call it the joy ?—of meeting you.'

'O fie, Mr. Guilfoyle ! were you actually flirting with her ?'

'Nay, pardon me ; I never flirt.'

'You were in love then ?'

'I was never in love till—'

A crash of notes as she resumed the air interrupted whatever he was about to say ; but his eye told more than his bold tongue would perhaps have dared to utter in such a time or place ; and, aware that they had met on the Continent, and had been for some time together in the seclusion of Craigaderyn, I began to fear that he must have far surpassed me in the chances of interest with her. Moreover, Dora's foolish remark might reasonably lead her to suppose that I was already involved with Winifred ; and now, with a somewhat cloudy expression in my face (as a mirror close by informed me), and a keen sense of pique in my heart, I listened while she played the accompaniment to his pretty long German song, the burden of which seemed to be ever and always—

'Ach nein ! ach nein ! ich darf es nich.
Leb' wohl ! Leb' wohl ! Leb' wohl !'

Sir Madoc, who had listened with some secret impatience to this most protracted German ditty, now begged his fair guest to favour him with something Welsh; but as she knew no airs pertaining to the locality, she resigned her place to Winifred, whom I led across the room, and by whose side I remained. After the showy performances of Lady Estelle, she was somewhat reluctant to begin : all the more so, perhaps, that her friend—with rather questionable taste, certainly—was wont, in a spirit of mischief or raillery—but one pardons so much in lovely woman, especially one of rank—to quiz Wales, its music and provincialism; just as, when in the Highlands, she had laughed at the natives, and voted 'their sham chiefs and gatherings as delightfully absurd.'

Finding that his daughter lingered ere she began, and half suspecting the cause, Sir Madoc threatened to send for Owen Gwyllim, the butler, with his harp. Owen had frequently accompanied her with his instrument ; but though that passed well enough occasionally among homely Welsh folks, it would never do when Lady Naseby and certain others were present.

'It is useless for an English girl to sing in a

foreign language, or attempt to rival paid profes-
sional artists, by mourning like Mario from the tur-
ret, or bawling like Edgardo in the burying-ground,
or to give us " Stride la vampa" in a fashion that
would terrify Alboni,' said Sir Madoc, 'or indeed to
attempt any of those operatic effusions with which
every hand organ has made us familiar. So come,
Winny, a Welsh air, or I shall ring for Owen.'

This rather blundering speech caused Lady
Estelle to smile, and Guilfoyle, whose 'Leb' wohl'
had been something of the style objected to,
coloured very perceptibly.

Thus urged, Winifred played and sang with
great spirit ' The March of the Men of Harlech ;'
doubtless as much to compliment Caradoc and me
as to please her father; for it was then our regimental march ; and, apart from its old Welsh
associations, it is one of the finest effusions of our
old harpers.

Sir Madoc beat time, while his eyes lit up
with enthusiasm, and he patted his daughter's
plump white shoulders kindly with his weather-
browned but handsome hands ; for the old gentleman rather despised gloves, indoors especially, as
effeminate.

Winifred had striven to please rather than to excel; and though tremulous at times, her voice was most attractive.

'Thank you,' said I, in a low and earnest tone; 'your execution is just of that peculiar kind which leaves nothing more to be wished for, and while it lasts, Winny, inspires a sense of joy in one's heart.'

'You flatter me much—far too much,' replied Miss Lloyd in a lower and still more tremulous tone, as she grew very pale; for some girls will do so, when others would flush with emotion, and it was evident that my praise gave her pleasure; she attached more to my words than they meant.

An undefinable feeling of pique now possessed me—a sensation of disappointment most difficult to describe; but it arose from a sense of doubt as to how I really stood in the estimation of the fair Estelle. Taking an opportunity, while Sir Madoc was emphatically discussing the points and pedigrees of certain horses and harriers with Guilfoyle and other male friends, while the Countess and other ladies were clustered about Winifred at the piano, and Dora and Caradoc were deep in some affair of their own, I leaned over her chair, and

referring—I forget now in what terms—to the last
time we met, or rather parted, I strove to effect
that most difficult of all moves in the game of
love—to lead back the emotions, or the past train
of thought, to where they had been dropped, or
snapped by mischance, to the time when I had
bid her lingeringly adieu, after duly shawling and
handing her to the carriage, at the close of a late
rout in Park-lane, when the birds of an early June
morning were twittering in the trees of Hyde Park,
when the purple shadows were lying deep about
the Serpentine, when the Ring-road was a solitude,
the distant Row a desert, and the yawning foot-
men in plush and powder, and the usually rubicund coachmen, looking weary, pale, and impa-
tient, and when the time and place were suited
neither for delay nor dalliance. Yet, as I have
elsewhere said, an avowal of all she had inspired
within me was trembling on my lips as I led her
through the marble vestibule and down the steps,
pressing her hand and arm the while against my
side; but her mother's voice from the depths of
the carriage (into which old Lord Pottersleigh
had just handed her) arrested a speech to which
she might only have responded by silence, then at

least; and I had driven, *via* Piccadilly, to the Junior U.S., when Westminster clock was paling out like a harvest moon beyond the Green Park, cursing my diffidence, that delayed all I had to say till the carriage was announced, thereby missing the chance that never might come again.

And then I had but the memory of a lovely face, framed by a carriage window, regarding me with a bright yet wistful smile, and of a soft thrilling pressure returned by an ungloved hand, that was waved to me from the same carriage as it rolled away westward.

The night had fled, and there remained of it only the memory of this, and of those glances so full of tenderness, and those soft attentions or half endearments which are so charming, and so implicitly understood, as almost to render language, perhaps, unnecessary.

'You remember the night we last met, and parted, in London?' I whispered.

'Morning, rather, I think it was,' said she, fanning herself; 'but night or morning, it was a most delightful ball. I had not enjoyed myself anywhere so much that season, and it was a gay one.'

'Ah, you have not forgotten it, then,' said I, encouraged.

'No; it stands out in my memory as one night among many happy ones. Day was almost breaking when you led me to the carriage, I remember.'

'Can you remember nothing more?' I asked earnestly.

'You shawled me most attentively—'

'And I was whispering—'

'Something foolish, no doubt; men are apt to do so at such times,' she replied, while her white eyelids quivered, and she looked up at me with her calm bright smile.

'Something foolish?' thought I reproachfully; 'and then, as now, my soul seemed on my lips.'

'Do you admire Mr. Guilfoyle's singing?' she asked after a little pause, to change the subject probably.

'His voice is unquestionably good and highly cultured,' said I, praising him truthfully enough to conceal the intense annoyance her unexpected question gave me; 'but, by the way, Lady Estelle, how does it come to pass that he has the honour of knowing you—to be *here*, too?'

'How—why—what *do* you mean, Mr. Hardinge?' she asked, and I could perceive that after colouring slightly she grew a trifle paler than before. 'He is a visitor here, like you or myself. We met him abroad first; he was most kind to us when mamma lost all her passports at the Berlin Eisenbahnhof, and he accompanied us to the Alte Leipziger Strasse for others, and saw us safely to our carriage. Then, by the most singular chances, we met him again at the new Kursaal of Ems, at Gerolstein, when we were beginning the tour of the Eifel, and at Baden-Baden. Lastly, we met him at Llandudno, on the beach, quite casually, when driving with Sir Madoc, to whom he said that he knew you—that you were quite old friends, in fact.'

'Knew me, by Jove! that is rather odd. I only lost some money to him; enough to make me wary for the future.'

'Wary?' she asked with dilated eyes.

'Yes.'

'An unpleasant expression, surely. Sir Madoc, who is so hospitable, asked him here to see the lions of Craigaderyn, and has put a gun at his disposal for the twelfth.'

'How kind of unthinking Sir Madoc! A most satisfactory explanation,' said I cloudily, while gnawing my moustache. Guilfoyle had too evidently followed them.

'If any explanation were necessary,' was the somewhat haughty response, as the mother-of-pearl fan went faster than ever, and she looked me full in the face with her clear, dark, and penetrating eyes, to the sparkle of which the form of their lids, and their thick fringe of black lash, served to impart a softness that was indeed required. 'Do you know anything of him?' she added.

'No; that is—'

'Anything against him?'

'No, Lady Estelle.'

'What then?' she asked, a little petulantly.

'Simply that I, pardon me, think a good deal.'

'More than you would say?'

'Perhaps.'

'This is not just. Mamma is somewhat particular, as you know; and our family solicitor, Mr. Sharpus, who is his legal friend also, speaks most warmly of him. We met him in the best society —abroad, of course; but, Mr. Hardinge, your words, your manner, more than all, your tone, imply what I fear Mr. Guilfoyle would strongly resent. But please go and be attentive to mamma —you have scarcely been near her to-night,' she added quickly, as a flush of anger crossed my face, and she perceived it.

I bowed and obeyed, with a smile on my lips and intense annoyance in my heart. I knew that the soft eyes of Winifred Lloyd had been on us from time to time; but my little flirtation with *her* was a thing of the past now, and I was reckless of its memory. Was she so? Time will prove.

I felt jealousy of Guilfoyle, pique at Lady Estelle, and rage at my own mismanagement. I had sought to resume the tenor of our thoughts and conversation on the occasion of our parting after that joyous and brilliant night in Park-lane, when my name on her engagement card had appeared thrice for that of any one else; but if I had touched her heart, even in the slightest degree, would she have become, as it seemed, almost warm in defence of this man, a waif picked up on the Continent? Yet, had she any deeper interest in him than mere acquaintanceship warranted, would she have spoken of him so openly, and so candidly, to me?

Heavens! we had actually been covertly fenc-
ing, and nearly quarrelling! Yet, if so, why
should she be anxious for me to win the estimation of 'mamma'?

Lady Naseby had been beautiful in her time,
and the utter vacuity and calm of her mind had
enabled her to retain much of that beauty unim-
paired; and I thought that her daughter, though
with more sparkle and brilliance, would be sure to
resemble her very much at the same years. She
was not displeased to meet with attention, but was
shrewd enough to see, and disdainful enough to
resent, its being bestowed, as she suspected it was
in my instance, on account of her daughter; thus
I never had much success; for on the night of that
very rout in London my attentions in that quarter,
and their apparent good fortune, had excited her
parental indignation and aristocratic prejudices
against me.

After all the visitors had withdrawn (as horses
or carriages were announced in succession), save
one or two fox-hunters whom Guilfoyle had lured
into the billiard-room for purposes of his own,
when the ladies left us at night Lady Estelle did
not give me her hand. She passed me with a bow

and smile only, and as she swept through the gilded folding doors of the outer drawing-room, with an arm round Dora's waist, her backward glances fell on all—but me.

Why was this? Was this coldness of manner the result of Guilfoyle's influence, fear of her mamma, her alleged engagement with old Lord Pottersleigh, pique at myself caused by Dora's folly, or what? It was the old story of 'trifles light as air.' I felt wrathful and heavy at heart, and repented bitterly the invitation I had accepted, and the leave I had asked; for Lady Estelle seemed so totally unconcerned and indifferent to me now, considering the *empressement* with which we had parted in London.

The 'family solicitor,' too! He had been introduced as a mutual friend in the course of affairs —in the course of a friendship that had ripened most wonderfully. Was this Hawkesby Guilfoyle a fool, or a charlatan, or both? His various versions of the diamond ring would seem to show that he was the former. What fancy had the Countess for him, and why was he tolerated by Sir Madoc? Familiar though I was with my old friend, I felt that I could not, without a violation of good taste,

ask a question about a guest, especially one introduced by the Cressinghams.

His voice was soft in tone; his manner, when
he chose, was suave; his laugh at all times, even
when he mocked and sneered, which was not un-,
frequent, silvery and pleasing; yet he was evidently one who could 'smile and smile and be'—I
shall not exactly say what.

While smoking a cigar, I pondered over these
and other perplexing things in my room before retiring for the night, hearing ever and anon the
click of the billiard-balls at the end of the corridor.
Had I not the same chance and right of competi-
tion as this Guilfoyle, though unknown to the
'family solicitor'? How far had he succeeded in
supplanting me, and perhaps others? for that
there were others I knew. How far had he gone
in his suit—how prospered? How was I to con-
strue the glances I had seen exchanged, the half
speech so bluntly made, and so adroitly drowned
at the piano? Who was he? what was he? The
attaché of the mock embassy at a petty German
Court! Surely my position in society was as
good, if not better defined than his; while youth,
appearance, health, and strength gave me every

advantage over an ' old fogie' like Viscount Pottersleigh.

As if farther to inflame my pique, and confirm
the chagrin and irritation that grew within me on
reflection, Phil Caradoc, smoothing his moustache,
came into my room, which adjoined his, to have,
as he said, ' a quiet weed before turning in.'

He looked ruffled ; for he had lost money at
billiards—that was evident—and to the object of
my jealousy, too.

'That fellow Guilfoyle is a thorough Bohemian,
if ever there was one !' said he, as he viciously bit
off the end of his cigar prior to lighting it, ' with
his inimitable tact, his steady stroke at billiards,
his scientific whist, his coolness and perfect breeding : yet he is, I am certain, unless greatly mistaken, a regular free-lance, without the bravery or
brilliance that appertained to the name of old—a
lawless ritter of the gaming-table, and one that
can't even act his part well or consistently in being
so. He has been spinning another story about
that ring, with which I suppose, like Claude Mel-
notte's, we shall hear in time his grandfather, the
Doge of Venice, married the Adriatic ! I am certain,' continued Caradoc, who was unusually ruf-

fled, 'that though a vainglorious and boasting fellow, he is half knave, half fool, and wholly adventurer!'

'This is strong language, Phil. Good heavens! do you really think so?' I asked, astonished to find him so boldly putting my own thoughts into words.

'I am all but convinced of it,' said he emphatically.

'But how in such society?'

'Ah, that is the rub, and the affair of Sir Madoc, and of Lady Naseby, and of Lady Estelle, too, for she seems to take rather more than an interest in him — they have some secret understanding. By Jove! I can't make it out at all!'

Caradoc's strong convictions and unusual bluntness added fuel to my pique and chagrin, and I resolved that, come what might, I would end the matter ere long; and I thought the while of the song of Montrose,

> 'He either fears his fate too much,
>   Or his deserts are small,
> Who dares not put it to the touch,
>   To gain or lose it all!'

CHAPTER VIII.

SUNDAY AT CRAIGADERYN.

THE following day was Sunday ; and ere it closed, there occurred a little contretemps which nearly lost me all chance of putting to the issue whether I was 'to gain or lose it all' with Estelle Cressingham.

I felt that it was quite possible, if I chose, to have my revenge through the sweet medium of Winifred Lloyd; yet, though Lady Estelle's somewhat pointed defence of Guilfoyle rankled in my memory, and Caradoc's hints had added fuel to the flame, I shrunk from such a double game, and hoped that the chances afforded by propinquity in general, and the coming fête in particular, would soon enable me to come to a decision. My mind was full of vague irritation against her ; yet when I rose in the morning, my one and predominant thought was that I should see her again.

Carriages and horses had been ordered from the stable for our conveyance to Craigaderyn church, a three miles' drive through lovely scenery, and I resolved to accompany the sisters in the barouche, leaving whom fate directed to take charge of Lady Estelle; yet great was my contentment when she fell to the care of Sir Madoc in the family carriage. Lady Naseby did not appear, her French soubrette, Mademoiselle Babette Pompon, announcing that she was indisposed.

Guilfoyle and Caradoc rode somewhat unwillingly together, and I sat opposite Winny, who insisted on driving, and was duly furnished with the smartest of parasol whips—pink, with a white fringe.

Quitting the park, we skirted a broad trout stream, the steep banks of which were clad with light-green foilage, and named *Nant-y-belan*, or the 'Martens' dingle.' At the bottom the river foamed along over broken and abutting rocks, or flowed in dark and noiseless pools, where the brown trout lurked in the shade, and where the over-arching trees and grassy knolls were reflected downward in the depth.

Hawkesby Guilfoyle sat his horse—one of Sir

Madoc's hunters, fully sixteen hands high—so well, and looked so handsome and gentlemanly, his riding costume was so complete, even to his silver spurs, well-fitting buff gloves, and riding switch, that I felt regret in the conviction that some cloud hung over the fellow's antecedents, and present life too perhaps; but with all that I could not forgive him his rivalry, and, as I deemed its presumption, with the strong belief that he was, in his secret heart, my enemy.

He and Caradoc rode behind the open carriage; we led the way in the barouche; and a very merry and laughing party we were, as we swept by the base of the green hills of Mynedd Hiraethrog, and over the ancient bridge that spans Llyn Aled, to the church of Craigaderyn, where the entrance of Sir Madoc's family and their visitors caused periodically somewhat of a sensation among the more humble parishioners who were there, and were wont to regard with a species of respectful awe the great square pew, which was lined with purple velvet, and had a carved-oak table in the centre, and over the principal seat the lion's head erased, and the shield of Lloyd per bend sinister, ermine and pean, a lion rampant, armed with a sword.

With a roof of carved oak, brought from some *other* place (the invariable account of all such roofs in Wales), and built by Jorwerth ap Davydd Lloyd, in 1320, the church was a picturesque old place, where many generations of the Craigaderyn family had worshipped long before and since the Reformation, and whose bones, lapped in lead, and even in coffins of stone, lay in the burial vaults below. The oaken pews were high and deep, and were covered with dates, coats-of-arms, and quaint monograms. In some places the white slabs indicated where lay the remains of those who died but yesterday. Elsewhere, with helmet, spurs, and gloves of steel hung above their stony effigies, and covered by cobwebs and dust, lay the men of ages past and gone, their brasses and pedestal tombs bearing, in some instances, how stoutly and valiantly they had fought against the Spaniard, the Frenchman, and the Scot.

One, Sir Madoc ap Meredyth Lloyd, whose sword hung immediately over my head, had wielded it, as his brass recorded, 'contra Scotos apud Flodden et Musselboro;' and now the spiders were busy spinning their cobwebs over the rusted helmet through which this old Welsh knight had seen

King James's host defile by the silver Till, and that of his fated granddaughter by the banks of the beautiful Esk.

In other places I saw the more humble, but curious Welsh mode of commemorating the dead, by hanging up a coffin-plate, inscribed with their names, in the pews where they were wont to sit.

Coats-of-arms met the eye on all sides—solid evidences of birth and family, which more than once evoked a covert sneer from Guilfoyle, who to his other bad qualities added the pride and the envy of such things, that seem inseparable from the character of the parvenu.

There were two services in Craigaderyn church each Sunday, one in Welsh, the other in English. Sir Madoc usually attended the former; but in courtesy to Lady Estelle, he had come to the latter to-day.

Over all the details of the village fane my eyes wandered from time to time, always to rest on the face of Estelle Cressingham or of Winifred Lloyd, who was beside me, and who on this day, as I had accompanied her, seemed to feel that she had me all to herself. We read off the same book, as we had done years before in the same pew and place;

ever and anon our gloved fingers touched; I felt
her silk dress rustling against me; her long lashes
and snowy lids, with the soft pale beauty of her
downcast face, and her sweetly curved mouth,
were all most pleasing and attractive; but the
sense of Estelle's presence rendered me invulner-
able to all but her; and my eyes could not but
roam to where she stood or knelt by the side of
burly Sir Madoc, her fine face downcast too in the
soft light that stole between the deep mullions and
twisted tracery of an ancient stained-glass window,
her noble and equally pure profile half seen and
half hidden by a short veil of black lace; her
rounded chin and lips rich in colour, and beautiful in character as those of one of Greuze's loveliest masterpieces. There too were the rich brightness of her hair, and the proud grace that per-
vaded all her actions, and even her stillness.

Thus, even when I did not look towards her,
but in Winifred's face, or on the book we mutually
held, and mechanically affected to read, a perception, a dreamy sense of Estelle's presence was
about me, and I could not help reverting to our
past season in London, and all that has been de-
scribed by a writer as those 'first sweet hours of

communion, when strangers glide into friends; that hour which, either in friendship or in love, is as the bloom to the fruit, as the daybreak to the day, indefinable, magical, and fleeting;' the hours which saw me presented as a friend, and left me a lover.

The day was intensely hot, and inside the old church, though some of the arched recesses and ancient tombs looked cool enough, there was a blaze of sunshine, that fell in hazy flakes or streams of coloured light athwart the bowed heads of the congregation. With heat and languor, there was also the buzz of insect life; and amid the monotonous tones of the preacher, I loved to fancy him reading the marriage service for us— that is, for Estelle and myself—fancied it as an enthusiastic school-girl might have done; and yet how was it that, amid these conceits, the face and form of Winifred Lloyd, with her pretty hand in the tight straw-coloured kid glove, that touched mine, filled up the eye of the mind?

Was I dreaming, or only about to sleep, like so many of the congregation—those toilers afield, those hardy hewers of wood and drawers of water, whose strong sinews, when unbraced, induced them

to slumber now—the men especially, as the study
of each other's toilets served to keep the female
portion fully awake.

When the clergyman prayed for the success of
our arms in the strife that was to come, Winifred's
dark eyes looked into mine for a moment, quick as
light, and I saw her bosom swell; and when he
prayed, 'Give peace in our time, O Lord,' her
voice became earnest and tremulous in responding;
and I could have sworn that I saw a tear oozing,
but arrested, on the thick black eyelash of this
impulsive Welsh girl, whom this part of the service, by its association and the time, seemed to
move; but Lady Estelle was wholly intent on having one of her gloves buttoned by Guilfoyle, whose
attendance she doubtless preferred to that of
old Sir Madoc.

'Look!' said Winifred Lloyd, in an excited
whisper, as she lightly touched my hand.

I followed the direction of her eye, and saw,
seated at the end of the central aisle, modestly
and humbly, among the free places reserved for
the poor, a young woman, whose appearance was
singularly interesting. Poorly, or rather plainly,
attired in faded black, her face was remarkably

handsome ; and her whole air was perfectly lady-
like.　She was as pale as death, with a wild wan
look in all her features ; disease, or sorrow, or
penury—perhaps all these together—had marked
her as their own ; her eyes, of clear, bright, and
most expressive gray, were haggard and hollow,
with dark circles under them.　Black-kid gloves
showed her pretensions to neatness and gentility ;
but as they were frayed and worn, she strove to
conceal her hands nervously under her gathered
shawl.

‘ She is looking at you, Winifred,’ said Dora.

‘ No—at Estelle.’

‘ At us all, I think,’ resumed Dora, in the same
whispered tone ; ‘ and she has done so for some
time past. Heavens ! she seems quite like a spectre.’

‘ Poor creature !’ said Winifred ; ‘ we must in-
quire about her.’

‘ Do you know her, Mr. Hardinge ?’ asked
Dora.

‘ Nay, not I ; it is Mr. Guilfoyle she is looking at,’ said I.

Guilfoyle, having achieved the somewhat protracted operation of buttoning Lady Estelle’s
lavender-kid glove, now stuck his glass in his

eye, and turned leisurely and languidly in the direction that attracted us all, just as the service was closing; but the pale woman quickly drew down her veil, and quitted the church abruptly, ere he could see her, as I thought; and this circumstance, though I took no heed of it then, I remembered in the time to come.

Winifred frankly took my arm as we left the church.

'You promised to come with me after luncheon and see the goat I have for the regiment,' said she.

'Did I?—ah, yes—shall be most happy, I'm sure,' said I, shamefully oblivious of the promise in question, as we proceeded towards the carriages, the people making way for us on all sides, the women curtseying and the men uncovering to Sir Madoc, who was a universal favourite, especially with the maternal portion of the parish, as he was very fond of children and flattered himself not a little on his power of getting on with them, being wont to stop mothers on the road or in the village street, and make knowing remarks on the beauty, the complexions, or the curly heads of their offspring, while he was never without a handful of copper or loose silver for general distribution; and

now it excited some surprise and even secret disdain in Guilfoyle—a little petulance in Lady Estelle too—to find him shaking hands and speaking
in guttural Welsh with some of the men cottagers,
or peasant-women with jackets and tall odd hats.
But one anecdote will suffice to show the character
of Sir Madoc.

In the very summer of my visit, it had occurred
that he had to serve on a jury when a property of
some three thousand pounds or so was at issue;
and when the jury retired, he found that they were
determined to decide in such a manner as he did
not deem equitable, and which in the end would
inevitably ruin an honest farmer named Evan
Rhuddlan, father of a sergeant in my company of
Welsh Fusileers, who dwelt at a place called Craig
Eryri, or 'the Rock of Eagles.' Finding that they
were resolute, he submitted, or affected to acquiesce
in their decision; but on announcing it to the
court, he handed the losing party a cheque on
Coutts and Co. for the whole sum in litigation,
and became more than ever the idol of the country
people.

'Romantic old place—casques, cobwebs, and
all that sort of thing,' said Guilfoyle, as he handed

Lady Estelle into the carriage, and took the bridle of his horse from Bob Spurrit, the groom; 'I thought Burke had written the epitaph of chivalry and all belonging to it.'

'Yes, but romance still exists, Mr. Guilfoyle,' said Winifred, whose face was bright with smiles.

'And love too, eh, Estelle?' added Dora, laughing.

'Even in the region of Mayfair, you think?' said she.

'Yes; and wherever there is beauty, that is rarest,' said I.

But she only replied by one of her calm smiles; for she had a reticence of manner which there seemed to be no means of moving.

'Talking of love and romance, I should like to know more of that pale woman we saw in church to-day,' said Dora.

'Why so?' asked Guilfoyle curtly.

'Because I saw she must have some terrible story to tell.—What was the text, Mr. Caradoc?' she asked, as we departed homewards.

'Haven't the ghost of an idea,' replied Phil.

'O fie!—or the subject?'

'No,' said Caradoc, reddening a little; for he

had been intent during the whole service on Winifred Lloyd.

'It was all about Jacob's ladder, of which we
have had a most inaccurate notion hitherto,' said
Dora, as we drove down the long lime avenue, to
find that, as the day was so sultry, luncheon had
been laid for us by Owen Gwyllim under the
grand old trees in the lawn, about thirty yards
from the entrance-hall, under the very oak where
the spectre of Sir Jorwerth Du was alleged to
vanish, the oak of Owen Glendower; and where
that doughty Cymbrian had perhaps sought to
summon spirits from the vasty deep, we found
spirits of another kind—brandy and seltzer, clicquot and sparkling moselle cooling in silver ice-
pails on the greensward; and there too, awaiting
us, sat Lady Naseby, smiling and fanning herself
under the umbrageous shadows of the chase.

Over her stately head was pinned a fall of rich
Maltese lace, that hung in lappets on each side
—a kind of demi-toilette that well became her
lingering beauty and matronly appearance.

In a mother-of-pearl basket by her side, and
placed on the luncheon-table, lay Tiny, her shock,
a diminutive cur, white as snow, spotless as Made-

moiselle Babette with perfumed soap could make
it, its long woolly hair dangling over its pink eyes,
giving it, as Sir Madoc said, 'a most pitiable
appearance;' for with all his love of dogs, he
disliked such pampered, waddling, and wheezing
pets as this, and thought manhood never looked
so utterly contemptible as when a tall 'Jeames'
in livery, with whiskers and calves, cane and
nosegay, had the custody of such a quadruped,
while his lady shopped in Regent-street or Piccadilly.

CHAPTER IX.

THE INITIALS.

WHILE we were at luncheon, and the swollen champagne-corks were flying upward into the green foliage overhead, and while Owen Gwyllim was supplying us with iced claret-cup from a great silver tankard presented to Sir Madoc's uncle by his regiment, the Ancient Britons, after the Irish rebellion of 1798, and with which he, Sir Madoc, had been wont to dispense swig or 'brown Betty' on St. David's-day, when at Cambridge, — Dora, with her hair flying loose, her eyes sparkling, and her face radiant with excitement and merriment, came tripping down the perron from the entrance-hall, and across the lawn towards us, with the contents of the household post-bag. She seemed to have letters for every one, save me—letters which she dropped and picked up as she came along. There was quite a pile of notes for herself, on the subject of her approaching fête; and how busy her pretty little hands immediately became!

After the usual muttered apologies, all began to read.

There was a letter for Guilfoyle, on reading which he grew very white, exhibited great trepidation, and thrust it into his coat-pocket.

'What is up, sir?' asked Sir Madoc, pausing with a slice of cold fowl on his fork; 'nothing unpleasant, I hope?'

'Sold on a bay mare—that is all,' he replied, with an affected laugh, as if to dismiss the subject.

'How?' asked Sir Madoc, whom a 'horsey' topic immediately interested.

'Like many other handicap "pots" this season, my nag came in worse than second.'

'A case of jockeying?'

'Pure and simple.'

'When?'

'O, ah—York races.'

'Why, man alive, they don't come off for a month yet!' responded Sir Madoc somewhat dryly; but perceiving that his guest was awkwardly placed, he changed the subject by saying, 'But your letter, Lady Estelle, gives you pleasure, I am glad to see.'

'It is from Lord Pottersleigh. He arrives here to-morrow, and hopes his rooms have a southern exposure.'

'The fête-day—of course. His comforts shall be fully attended to.'

'Why did he write to *her* about this, and not to Sir Madoc or Miss Lloyd ?' thought I.

'He is such an old friend,' remarked Lady Estelle, as if she divined my mental query.

'Yes, rather too old for my taste,' said the somewhat mischievous Dora. 'He wears goloshes in damp weather, his hat down on the nape of his neck; is in an agony of mind about exposures, draughts, and currents of air; makes his horse shy every time he attempts to mount, and they go round in circles, eyeing each other suspiciously till a groom comes ; and when he does achieve his saddle, he drops his whip or his gloves, or twists his stirrup-leather. And yet it is this old fogie whose drag at Epsom or the Derby makes the greatest show, has the finest display of lovely faces, fans, bonnets, and parasols — a moving

Swan and Edgar, with a luncheon spread that Fortnum and Mason might envy, and champagne flowing as if from a fountain ; but withal, he is so tiresome !'

'Dora, you quite forget yourself,' said Winifred, while I could have kissed her for this sketch of my rival, at which Sir Madoc, and even Estelle Cressingham, laughed ; but Lady Naseby said, with some asperity of tone,

'Lord Pottersleigh is one of our richest peers, Miss Dora, and his creation dates from Henry VIII.'

'And he is to dance with me,' said the heedless girl, still laughing. 'O, won't I astonish his nerves if we waltz !'

'Your cousin Naseby is to visit us, Estelle, at Walcot Park, so soon as we return, if he can,' said the Countess, turning from Dora with a very dubious expression of eye, and closing a letter she had received ; 'his love-affair with that odious Irish girl is quite off, thank heaven !'

'How ?—love of change, or change of love ?'

'Neither.'

'What, then, mamma ?'

'The Irish girl actually had a mind of her

own, and preferred some one else even to a peer, an English peer!'

'I drain this clicquot to the young lady's happiness,' said Sir Madoc.

'But all this is nothing to me, mamma,' said Lady Estelle coldly.

But I could see at a glance, that if it was unimportant to *her*, it was not so to her mother, his aunt, who would rather have had the young earl for her son-in-law than the old viscount, even though the patent of the latter had been expede by the royal Bluebeard, most probably for services that pertained more to knavery than knighthood.

'Well, Caradoc,' said I, 'is your despatch from the regiment?'

'Yes; from Price of ours. Nothing but rumours of drafts going eastward to make up the death-losses at Varna, and he fears our leave may be cancelled. "Deuced awkward if we go soon," he adds, "as I have a most successful *affaire du cœur* on hand just now."'

'When is he ever without one?' said I; and we both laughed.

Winifred's eyes were on me, and Caradoc's were on her, while I was sedulously attending to

Lady Estelle. As for Guilfoyle, since the advent of his letter he had become quite silent. We were at the old game of cross-purposes; for it seems to be in love, as with everything else in life, that the obstacles in the way, and the difficulty of attainment, always enhance the value of the object to be won. Yet in the instance of Lady Estelle I was not so foolish as poor Price of ours, the butt of the mess, who always fell in love with the wrong person—to whom the pale widow, inconsolable in her first crape; the blooming bride in her clouds of tulle and white lace; the girl just engaged, and who consequently saw but one man in the world, and that man her own *fiancé;* or any pretty girl whom he met just when the route came and the mess-plate was packed prior to marching, —became invested with remarkable charms, and a sudden interest that made his susceptible heart feel sad and tender.

The ladies' letters opened up quite a budget of town news and gossip. To Sir Madoc, a genuine country gentleman, full only of field-sports, the prospects of the turnip crop and the grouse season, the county-pack, and so forth, a conversation that now rose, chiefly on the coming fête, on dresses, music, routs and Rotten-row, kettledrums and drawing-rooms, and the town in general, proved somewhat of a bore. He fidgeted, and ultimately left for the stables, where he and Bob Spurrit had to hold a grave consultation on certain equine ailments. The ladies also rose to leave us; but Caradoc, Guilfoyle, and I lingered under the cool shadow of the oaks, and lit our cigars. With his silver case for holding the last-named luxuries, Guilfoyle unconsciously pulled forth a letter, which fell on the grass at my feet. Picking it up, I restored it to him; but brief though the action, I could not help perceiving it to be the letter he had just received, that it was addressed in a woman's hand, and had on the envelope, in coloured letters, the name 'Georgette.'

'Thanks,' said he, with sudden irritation of manner, as he thrust it into a breast-pocket this time; 'a narrow squeak that!' he added slangily, with a half-muttered malediction.

I felt certain that there was a mystery in all this; that he feared something unpleasant might have been revealed, had that identical letter fallen into *other* hands, or under more prying eyes; and I remembered those trivial circumstances at a

future, and to me rather harassing, time. I
must own that this man was to me a puzzle.
With all his disposition to boast, he never spoke
of relations or of family; yet he seemed in perfectly easy circumstances; his own valet, groom,
and horses were at Craigaderyn; he could bear
himself well and with perfect ease in the best
society; and it was evident that, wherever they
came from, he was at present a man of pretty
ample means. He possessed, moreover, a keen
perception for appreciating individuals and events
at their actual value; his manners were, *when he
chose*, polished, his coolness imperturbable, and
his *insouciance* sometimes amusing. For the present, it had left him.

'Beautiful brilliant that of yours, Mr. Guilfoyle,' said Caradoc, to fish for another legend of
the ring; but in vain, for Guilfoyle was no longer
quite himself, though he had policy enough to
feed the snarling cur Tiny in her basket, with
choice morsels of cold fowl, as Lady Naseby's
soubrette, Mademoiselle Babette, was waiting to
carry it away.

Since the remarks or *contretemps* concerning
the York races, he had been as mute as a fish;

and now, when he did begin to speak in the absence of Sir Madoc, I could perceive that gratitude
for kindness did not form an ingredient in the
strange compound of which his character was
made up. Perhaps secret irritation at Sir Madoc's
queries about the letter which so evidently dis-
turbed his usual equanimity might have been the
real spirit that moved him now to sneer at the
old baronet's Welsh foibles, and particularly his
weakness on the subject of pedigrees.

'You are to stay here for the 1st, I believe?'
said I.

'Yes; but, the dooce! for what? Such a la-
bour to march through miles of beans and growing
crop, to knock over a few partridges and rabbits'
(partwidges and wabbits, he called them), 'which
you can pay another to do much better for you.'

'Sturdy Sir Madoc would hear this with in-
credulous astonishment,' said I.

'Very probably. Kind fellow old Taffy,
though,' said he, while smoking leisurely, and
lounging back in an easy garden-chair; 'has a
long pedigree, of course, as we may always remember by the coats-of-arms stuck up all over the
house. "County people" in the days of Howel

Dha; "county ditto" in the days of Queen Victoria, and likely to remain so till the next flood forms a second great epoch in the family history. Very funny, is it not? He reminds me of what we read of Mathew Bramble in *Humphry Clinker*—a gentleman of great worth and property, descended in a straight line by the female side from Llewellyn, Prince of Wales.'

I was full of indignation on hearing my old friend spoken of thus, if not under his own roof, under his ancient ancestral oaks; but Philip Caradoc, more Celtic and fiery by nature, anticipated me by saying sharply,

'Bad taste this, surely, in you, Mr. Guilfoyle, to sneer thus at our hospitable entertainer; and believe me, sir, that no one treats lightly the pedigree of another who—who—'

'Ah, well—who what?'

'Possesses one himself,' added Phil, looking him steadily in the face.

'Bah! I suppose every one has had a grandfather.'

'Even you, Mr. Guilfoyle?' continued Caradoc, whose cheek began to flush; but the other replied calmly, and not without point,

'There is a writer who says, that to pride

oneself on the nobility of one's ancestors is like
looking among the roots for the fruit that should
be found on the branches.'

Finding that the conversation was taking a
decidedly unpleasant turn, and that, though his
tone was quiet and his manner suave, a glassy
glare shone in the greenish-gray eyes of Guilfoyle,
I said, with an assumed laugh,

'We must not forget the inborn ideas and the
national sentiments of the Welsh—call them pro-
vincialisms if you will.   But remember that there
are eight hundred thousand people inspired by a
nationality so strong, that they will speak only the
language of the Cymri; and it is among those
chiefly that our regiment has ever been recruited.
But if the foibles—I cannot deem them folly—of
Sir Madoc are distasteful to you, the charms of
the scenery around us and those of our lady friends
cannot but be pleasing.'

'Granted,' said he coldly; 'all are beautiful,
even to Miss Dora, who looks so innocent.'

'Who *is* so innocent by nature, Mr. Guilfoyle,'
said I, in a tone of undisguised sternness.

'Then it is a pity she permits herself to say—
sharp things.'

'With so much unintentional point, perhaps?'

' Sir !'

' Truth, then—which you will,' said I, as we simultaneously rose to leave the luncheon-table.

And now, oddly enough, followed by Winifred, Dora herself came again tripping down the broad steps of the perron towards us, exclaiming,

'Is not papa with you ?—the tiresome old dear, he will be among the harriers or the stables of course !'

'What is the matter ?' I asked.

' Only think, Mr. Hardinge, that poor woman we saw at church this morning, looking so pretty, so pale, and interesting, was found among the tombstones by Farmer Rhuddlan, quite in a helpless faint, after we drove away—so the housekeeper tells me; so we must find her out and succour her if possible.'

' But who is she ?' asked Caradoc.

' No one knows; she refused obstinately to give her name or tell her story ere she went away; but at her neck hangs a gold locket, with a crest, the date, 1st of September, on one side, and H. G. beautifully enamelled on the other. How odd— your initials, Mr. Guilfoyle !'

'You are perhaps not aware that my name is Henry Hawkesby Guilfoyle,' said he with ill-

concealed anger, while he played nervously with
his diamond ring.

'How intensely odd!' resumed his beautiful
but unwitting tormentor; 'H. H. G. were the
three letters on the locket!'

'Did no one open it?' he asked.

'No; it was firmly closed.'

'By a secret spring, no doubt.'

Guilfoyle looked ghastly for a moment, or it
might have been the effect of the sunlight flashing
on his face through the waving foliage of the trees
overhead; but he said laughingly,

'A droll coincidence, which, under some circumstances, might be very romantic, but fortunately in the present has no point whatever. If
my initials hung at your neck instead of hers,
how happy I should be, Miss Dora!'

And turning the matter thus, by a somewhat
clumsy compliment or bit of flattery, he ended an
unpleasant conversation by entering the house
with her and Caradoc.

Winifred remained irresolutely behind them.

'We were to visit my future comrade,' said I.

'Come, then,' said she, with a beautiful smile,
and a soft blush of innocent pleasure.

CHAPTER X.

WINIFRED LLOYD was, as Caradoc had said, a very complete and perfect creature. The very way her gloves fitted, the handsome form of her feet, the softness of her dark eyes, the tender curve of her lips, and, more than all, her winning manner—the inspiration of an innocent and guileless heart—made her a most desirable companion at all times; but with me, at present, poor Winifred was only the means to an end; and perhaps she secretly felt this, as she lingered pensively for a moment by the marble fountain that stood before Craigaderyn Court, and played with her white fingers in the water, causing the gold and silver fish to dart madly to and fro.

Above its basin a group of green bronze tritons were spouting, great Nile lilies floated on its surface, and over all was the crest of the Lloyds, also in bronze, a lion's head, gorged, with a wreath of oak.

The notes of a harp came softly towards us through the trees as we walked onward, for old Owen Gwyllim the butler was playing in that most unromantic place his pantry, and the air was the inevitable 'Jenny Jones.'

From the lawn I led her by walks and ways forgotten since my boyhood, and since I had gone the same route with her birdnesting and nutting in those glorious Welsh woods, by hedgerows that were matted and interwoven with thorny brambles and bright wild-flowers, past laden orchards and picturesque farms, nooks that were leafy and green, and little tarns of gleaming water, that reflected the smiling summer sky; past meadows, where the sleek brown, or black, or brindled cattle were chewing the cud and ruminating knee-deep among the fragrant pasture; and dreamily I walked by her side, touching her hand from time to time, or taking it fairly in mine as of old, and occasionally enforcing what I said by a pressure of her soft arm within mine, while I talked to her, saying heaven knows what, but most ungratefully

wishing all the time that she were Estelle Cressingham.

All was soft and peaceful around us. The
woods of Craigaderyn, glowing in the heat of the
August afternoon, were hushed and still, all save
the hum of insects, or if they stirred it was when
the soft west wind seemed to pass through them
with a languid sigh; and so some of the influences
of a past time and a boyish love came over me;
a time long before I had met the dazzling Estelle
—a time when to me there had seemed to be but
one girl in the world, and she was Winifred
Lloyd—ere I joined the —th in the West Indies,
or the Welsh Fusileers, and knew what the
world is.

I dreaded being betrayed into some tenderness
as a treason to Lady Estelle; and fortunately we
were not without some interruptions in our walk
of a mile or so to visit her horned pet, whom she
had sent forth for a last run on his native hills.

We visited Yr Ogof (or the cave) where one of
her cavalier ancestors had hidden after the battle
of Llandegai, in the Vale of the Ogwen, during
the wars of Cromwell, and now, by local superstition, deemed an abode of the knockers, those

supernatural guardians of the mines, to whom are known all the metallic riches of the mountains; hideous pigmy gnomes, who, though they can never be seen, are frequently heard beating, blasting, and boring with their little hammers, and singing in a language known to themselves only. Then we tarried by the heaped-up cairn that marked some long-forgotten strife; and then by the Maen Hir, a long boulder, under which some fabled giant lay; and next a great rocking stone, amid a field of beans, which we found Farmer Rhuddlan — a sturdy specimen of a Welsh Celt, high cheek-boned and sharp-eyed—contemplating with great satisfaction.

High above the sea of green stalks towered that wizard altar, where whilom an archdruid had sat, and offered up the blood of his fellow-men to gods whose names and rites are alike buried in oblivion; but Strabo tells us that it was from the flowing blood of the victim that the Druidesses— virgins supposed to be endowed with the gift of prophecy—divined the events of the future; and this old stone, now deemed but a barrier to the plough, had witnessed those terrible observances.

Poised one block upon the other, resting on the space a sparrow alone might occupy, and having stood balanced thus mysteriously for uncounted ages, lay the rocking stone. The farmer applied his strong hand to the spheroidal mass, and after one or two impulses it swayed most perceptibly. Then begging me not to forget his son, who was with our Fusileers far away at Varna, he respectfully uncovered his old white head, and left us to continue his tour of the crops, but not without bestowing upon us a peculiar and knowing smile, that made the blood mantle in the peachlike cheeks of Winifred.

'How strange are the reflections these solemn old relics excite!' said she somewhat hastily; 'if, indeed, one may pretend to value or to think of such things in these days of ours, when picturesque superstition is dying, and poetry is long since dead.'

'Poetry dead?'

'I think it died with Byron.'

'Poetry can never die while beauty exists,' said I, smiling rather pointedly in her face.

My mind being so filled with Estelle and her fancied image, caused me to be unusually soft and tender to Winifred. I seemed to be mingling one woman's presence with that of another. I regarded Winifred as the dearest of friends; but I loved Estelle with a passion that was full of enthusiasm and admiration.

'No two men have the same idea of beauty,' said Winifred after a pause.

'True, nor any two nations; it exists chiefly, perhaps, in the mind of the lover.'

'Yet love has nothing exactly to do with it.'

'Prove this,' said I, laughing as I caught her hand in mine.

'Easily. Ask a Chinese his idea of loveliness, and he will tell you, a woman with her eyebrows plucked out, the lids painted, her teeth blackened, and her feet shapeless; and what does the cynical Voltaire say?—"Ask a toad what is beauty, the supremely beautiful, and he will answer you, it is his female, with two round eyes projecting out of its little head, a broad flat neck, a yellow breast, and dark-brown back"? Even red hair is thought lovely by some; and did not Duke Philip the Good institute the order of the Golden Fleece of Burgundy in honour of a damsel whose hair was as yellow as saffron; and now, Harry Hardinge, what is *your* idea?'

'Can you ask me?' I exclaimed with something of ardour, for she looked so laughingly bright and intelligent as she spoke; then divining that I was thinking of another, not of her, 'for there is a thread in our thoughts even as there is a pulse in our hearts, and he who can hold the one knows how to think, and he who can move the other knows how to feel,' she said, with a point scarcely meant,

'The eye may be pleased, the vanity flattered, and ambition excited by a woman of beauty, especially if she is one of rank; yet the heart may be won by one her inferior. Talking of beauty, Lady Naseby has striven hard to get the young earl, her nephew, to marry our friend, Lady Estelle.'

'Would she have him?' I asked, while my cheek grew hot.

'I cannot say—but he declined,' replied Winifred, pressing a wild rose to her nostrils.

'Declined—impossible!'

'Why impossible? But in her fiery pride Estelle will never, never forgive him; though he was already engaged to one whom he, then at least, loved well.'

'Ah—the Irish girl, I suppose?'

'Yes,' said Winifred, with a short little sigh, as she looked down.

'Such a girl as Estelle Cressingham must always find admirers.'

'Hundreds; but as the estates, like the title, have passed to the next male heir, and Lady Naseby has only a life-rent of the jointure house in Hants—Walcot Park, a lovely place—she is anxious that her daughter should make a most suitable marriage.'

'Which means lots of tin, I suppose?' said I sourly.

'Exactly,' responded Winifred, determined, perhaps, if I had the bad taste to speak so much of Estelle, to say unpleasant things; 'and the favoured *parti* at present is Viscount Pottersleigh, who comes here to-morrow, as his letter informed her.'

'Old Pottersleigh is sixty if he is a day!' said I emphatically.

'What has age to do with the matter in view? Money and position are preferable to all fancies of the heart, I fear.'

'Nay, nay, Winifred, you belie yourself and Lady Estelle too; love is before everything!'

She laughed at my energy, while I began to feel that, next to making love, there is nothing so pleasant or so suggestive as talking of it to a pretty girl; and I beg to assure you, that it was somewhat perilous work with one like Winifred Lloyd; a girl who had the sweetest voice, the most brilliant complexion, and the softest eyes perhaps in all North Wales. She now drew her hand away; till then I had half forgot it was *her* hand I had been holding.

'Remember that oft-quoted line in the song of Montrose,' said she, pretty pointedly.

'Which? for I haven't an idea.'

'"Love *one*—and love no more."'

'The great marquis was wrong,' said I; 'at least, if, according to a more obscure authority in such matters, Price of ours, one may love many times and always truly.'

'Indeed!' Her lip curled as she spoke.

'Yes; for may not the same charms, traits, manner, and beauty which lure us to love once, lure us to love again?'

Winifred actually sighed, with something very like irritation, as she said,

'I think all this the most abominable sophis-
try, Mr. Hardinge, and I feel a hatred for " Price
of ours," whoever he may be.'

'Mister !   Why I was Harry a moment ago.'

'Well, here is the abode of Carneydd Llewellyn ; and you must tell me what you think of
your future Welsh comrade ; his beard may be
to the regimental pattern, though decidedly his
horns and moustaches are not.'

As she said this, again laughingly, we found
ourselves close to a little hut that abutted on a
thatched cottage and cow-house, in a most secluded place, a little glen or dell, over which the
trees were arching, and so forming a vista, through
which we saw Craigaderyn Court, as if in a frame
of foliage.

She opened a little wicket, and at the sound of
her voice the goat came forth, dancing on his hind
legs—a trick she had taught him—or playfully
butting her skirts with his horns, regarding me
somewhat dubiously and suspiciously the while
with his great hazel eyes.

He was truly a splendid specimen of the old
Carnarvonshire breed of goats, which once ran
wild over the mountains there, and were either

hunted by dogs or shot with the bullet so lately as Pennant's time. His hair, which was longer than is usual with those of England, led me to fancy there was a Cashmerian cross in his blood; his black horns were two feet three inches long, and more than two feet from one sharp tip to the other. He was as white as the new-fallen snow, with a black streak down the back, and his beard was as venerable in proportion and volume as it was silky in texture.

'He is indeed a beautiful creature—a noble fellow!' I exclaimed with genuine admiration.

'And just four years old. I obtained him when quite a kid.'

'I am so loth that the Fusileers should deprive you of him.'

'Talk not of that; but when you see my goat, my old pet Carneydd Llewellyn, marching proudly at their head, and decked with chaplets on St. David's day, when you are far, far away from us, you will—' she paused.

'What, Winifred?'

'Think sometimes of Craigaderyn—of to-day —and of me, perhaps,' she added, with a laugh that sounded strangely unlike one.

'Do I require aught to make me think of you?' said I, patting kindly the plump ungloved hand with which she was caressing the goat's head, and which in whiteness rivalled the hue of his glossy coat; and thereon I saw a Conway pearl, in a ring I had given her long ago, when she was quite a little girl.

'I hope not—and papa—I hope not.'

The bright beaming face was upturned to me, and, as the deuce would have it, I kissed her: the impulse was irresistible.

She trembled then, withdrew a pace or two, grew very pale, and her eyes filled with tears.

'You should not have done that, Harry—I mean, Mr. Hardinge.'

There was something wild and pitiful in her face.

'Tears?' said I, not knowing very well what to say; for 'people often *do* say very little, when they mean a great deal.'

'My old favourite will know the black ladders of Carneydd Llewellyn no more,' said she, stooping over the goat caressingly to hide her confusion.

'But, Winifred—Miss Lloyd—why tears?'

'Can you ask me?' said she, her eyes flashing through them.

'Why, what a fuss you make! I have often done so—when a boy!'

'But you are no longer a boy; nor am I a girl, Mr. Hardinge.'

'Do please call me Harry, like Sir Madoc,' I entreated.

'Not now—after this; and here comes Lady Estelle.'

'Estelle!'

At that moment, not far from us, we saw Lady Naseby, driven in a pony-phaeton by Caradoc, and Lady Estelle with Guilfoyle a little way behind them, on horseback, and unaccompanied by any groom, coming sweeping at a trot down the wooded glen.

Such is the amusing inconsistency of the human heart—the male human heart, perhaps my lady readers will say—that though I had been more than flirting with Winifred Lloyd—on the eve of becoming too tender, perhaps—I felt a pang of jealousy on seeing that Guilfoyle was Lady Estelle's sole companion, for Dora was doubtless immersed in the details of her forthcoming fête.

Had she seen us?

Had she detected in the distance that little

salute? If so, in the silly, kindly, half-flirting, and half-affectionate impulse which led me to kiss my beautiful companion and playfellow of the past years—the mere impulse of a moment—if mistaken, I might have ruined myself with her—perhaps with both.

'A lovely animal! I hope you are gratified, Mr. Hardinge?' said Lady Estelle, with—but perhaps it was fancy—a curl on her red lip, as she reined-in her spirited horse sharply with one firm hand, and caressed his arching neck gracefully with the other, while he rose on his hind legs, and her veil flew aside.

Already dread of the future had chased away my first emotion of pique, nor was it possible to be long angry with Estelle; for with men and women alike, her beauty made her irresistible. Some enemies among the latter she undoubtedly had; they might condemn the regularity of her features as too classically severe, or have said that at times the flash of her dark eyes was proud or defiant; but the smile that played about her lip was so soft and winning, that its influence was felt by all.

Her perfect ease of manner seemed cold—very cold indeed—when compared to the thoughts that burned in my own breast at that moment—dread that I might have been trifling with Winifred Lloyd, for whom I cherished a sincere and tender friendship; intense annoyance lest my friend Caradoc, who really loved her, might resent the affair; and, more than all, that she for whom I would freely have perilled limb and life might also resent, or mistake, the situation entirely.

And in this vague mood of mind I returned with the little party to the house, where the bell had rung for tea, before dinner, which was always served at eight o'clock. As we quitted the goat, its keeper, an old peasant dame, wearing a man's hat and coat, with a striped petticoat and large spotted handkerchief, looked affectionately after Miss Lloyd, and uttered an exclamation in Welsh, which Caradoc translated to me as being,

'God bless her! May feet so light and pretty never carry a heavy heart!'

CHAPTER XI.

THE FETE CHAMPETRE.

How wild and inconceivable, abrupt, yet quite practicable, were the brilliant visions I drew, the projects I formed! Mentally I sprang over all barriers, cleared at a flying leap every obstacle. In fancy I achieved all my desires. I was the husband of Estelle; the chosen son-in-law of her mother—the man of all men to whom she would have intrusted the future happiness of her only daughter. The good old lady had sacrificed pride, ambition, and all to love. Time, life-usage, all became subservient to me when in these victorious moods. I had distanced all rivals—she was mine; I hers. I had cut the service, bidden farewell to the Royal Welsh; she, for a time at least, to London, the court, the Row, 'society,' the world itself for me; and were rusticating, hand-in-hand, amid the woods of Walcot Park, or somewhere else, of which I had a very vague idea. But from these day-dreams, I had to rouse myself to the knowledge that, so far from being accepted, I had not yet ventured to propose; that I had more than one formidable rival; that other obstacles were to be overcome; and that Lady Naseby was as cold and proud and unapproachable as ever.

The day of Dora's fête proved a lovely one. The merry little creature—for she was much less in stature than her elder sister—with her bright blue eyes and wealth of golden hair, was full of smiles, pleasure, and impatience; and was as radiant with gems, the gifts of friends, as a young bride. I welcomed the day with vague hopes that grew into confidence, though I could scarcely foresee how it was to close for me, or all that was to happen.

Though Caradoc and I had come from Winchester ostensibly to attend this fête, I must glance briefly at many of the details of it, and confine myself almost to the *dramatis personæ*. Suffice it to say, that there was a militia band on one of the flower-terraces; there was a pretty dark-eyed Welsh gipsy, with black dishevelled hair, who told fortunes, and picked up, but omitted to restore, certain stray spoons and forks; there was an itinerant Welsh harper, whom the stag-hound Brach, the same stately animal which I had seen on the rug before the hall-fire, inspired by that animosity which all dogs seem to have for mendicants, assailed about the calf of the leg, for which he seemed to have a particular fancy. So Sir Madoc had to plaster the bite with a fifty-pound note. Then there was a prophetic hermit, in a moss-covered grotto, cloaked like a gray friar, and bearded like the pard; a wizard yclept Merlin, who, having imbibed too much brandy, made a great muddle of the predictions and couplets so carefully intrusted to him for judicious utterance; and who assigned the initials of Lady Estelle Cressingham to the portly old vicar, as those of his future spouse, and those of his lady, a stout matron with eight bantlings, to me, and so on.

The company poured in fast; and after being duly received by Sir Madoc and Miss Lloyd in the great drawing-room, literally crowded all the beautiful grounds, the band in white uniform on the terrace being a rival attraction to the great refreshment tent or marquee—a stately poly-

chromed edifice, with gilt bells hanging from each
point of the vandyked edging—wherein a standing
luncheon was arranged, under the care of Owen
Gwyllim ; and over all floated a great banner, ermine and pean, with the lion rampant of the Lloyds.

A ball was to follow in the evening. The floor
of the old dining-hall had been waxed till it shone
like glass for the dancers. Its walls were hung
with evergreens and coloured lamps, and a select
few were invited ; but Fate ordained that neither
Lady Estelle nor I were to figure in this, the
closing portion of the festivities.

A number of beautiful girls in charming toilettes were present. People of the best style too
mingled with humble middle-class country folks—
tenants and so forth. There were some officers
from the detachments quartered in Chester, and
several little half-known parsons, in Noah's-ark
coats, who came sidling in, and intrenched themselves beside huge mammas in quiet corners, to
discuss parish matters and general philanthropy
through the medium of iced claret-cup and sparkling moselle. And there were present too, as Guilfoyle phrased it, ' some of those d—d fellows who
write and paint, by Jove !'

On this day Guilfoyle, though he had carefully attired himself in correct morning costume, seemed rather preoccupied and irritable. The presence of Pottersleigh and so many others placed his society somewhat at a discount; and, glass in eye, he seemed to watch the arrival of the lady guests, especially any who were darkly attired, with a nervous anxiety, which, somehow, I mentally connected with the pale woman in church, and Dora's story of the initials.

There was undoubtedly some mystery about him.

Viewed from the perron of the house, the scene was certainly a gay one—the greenness of the closely-mown lawn, dotted by the bright costumes of the ladies, and a few scarlet coats (among them Caradoc's and mine); the brilliance and the perfume of flowers were there; the buzz of happy voices, the soft laughter of well-bred women, and the strains of the band, as they ebbed and flowed on the gentle breeze of the sunny noon.

Every way it was most enjoyable. Here on one side spread an English chase, with oaks as old perhaps as the days when 'Beddgelert heard the bugle sound,' leafy, crisp, and massive, their shadows casting a tint that was almost blue on the soft greensward, with the sea rippling and sparkling about a mile distant, where a portion of the chase ended at the edge of some lofty cliffs. On the other side rose the Welsh mountains, with all their gray rocks, huge boulders, and foaming waterfalls—mountains from where there seemed in fancy to come the scent of wild flowers, of gorse and blackberries, to dispel the fashionable languor of the promenaders on the lawn. The leaves, the flowers, the trees of the chase, the ladies' dresses, and the quaint façade of the old Tudor mansion were all warm with sunshine.

Old Morgan Roots the gardener, to his great disgust, had been compelled to rifle the treasures of his hothouses, and to strip his shelves of the most wonderful exotics, to furnish bouquets for the ladies ; for Morgan was proud of his floral effects, and when displaying his slippings from Kew and all the best gardens in England, tulips from Holland and the Cape, peonies from Persia, rhododendrons from Asia, azaleas from America, wax-like magnolias, and so forth, he was wont to exult over his rival, the vicar's Scotch gardener, whom he stigmatised as ' a sassenach ;' and not the least of his efforts were some superb roses, named 'the Dora,' in honour of the fair-haired heroine of the day.

And Caradoc—who was a good judge of every-thing, from cutlets and clicquot to horses and harness, and had a special eye for ankles, insteps, and eyelashes, style and colour, &c.—declared the fête to be quite a success.

As I looked around me, I could not but feel how England is preëminently, beyond all others, the land of fair women and of beauty. Lady Estelle, with her pale complexion and thick dark hair, her dress of light-blue silk, over which she wore a white transparent tunique, her tiny bonnet of white lace, her gloves and parasol of the palest silver-gray, seemed a very perfect specimen of her class; but until Lord Pottersleigh appeared, which was long after dancing had begun on the sward (by country visitors chiefly), she sat by the side of mamma, and declined all offers from partners.

The Viscount—my principal *bête noire*—had arrived over-night in his own carriage from Chester, but did not appear at breakfast next morning, nor until fully midday, as he had to pass —so Dora whispered to me—several hours in an arm-chair, with his gouty feet enveloped in flannel, while he regaled himself by sipping colchicum and warm wine-whey, though he alleged that his lameness was caused by a kick from his horse; and now, when with hobbling steps he came to where Lady Naseby and her stately daughter were seated, he did not seem—his coronet and Order of the Garter excepted—a rival to be much dreaded by a smart Welsh Fusileer of five-and-twenty.

Fully in his sixtieth year, and considerably wasted—more perhaps by early dissipation than by time—the Viscount was a pale, thin, and feeble-looking man, hollow-chested and slightly bent, with an unsteadiness of gait, an occasional querulousness of manner and restlessness of eye, as if nervous of the approach of many of those among whom he now found himself, and whom he viewed as 'bumpkins in a state of rude health.' Guilfoyle, of whom he evidently had misgivings, he regarded with a cold and aristocratic stare, after carefully adjusting a gold eyeglass on his thin aquiline nose, and yet they had been twice introduced elsewhere.

His features were good. In youth he had been deemed a handsome man; but now his brilliant teeth were of Paris, and what remained of his hair was carefully dyed a clear dark brown, that consorted but ill with the wrinkled aspect of his face, and the withered appearance of his thin white hands, when he ungloved, which was seldom. His whole air and style were so different from those of hearty and jolly Sir Madoc, whose years were the same, and who was looking so bland, so bald and shiny in face and brow, so full and round in waistcoat, with one of the finest camellias in his button-hole, 'just like Morgan Roots the gardener going to church on Sunday,' as Dora had it, while he watched the dancers, and clapped his hands to the music.

'Ha, Pottersleigh,' said he, 'you and I have done with this sort of thing now; but I have seen the day, when I was young, less fleshy, and didn't ride with a crupper, I could whirl in the waltz like a spinning jenny.'

To this awkward speech the Viscount, who affected juvenility, responded by a cold smile; and as he approached and was welcomed by Lady Naseby and her daughter, the latter glanced at me, and I could detect an undefinable expression, that savoured of amusement, or disdain, or annoyance, or all together, ending with a haughty smile, hovering on her dark and ever-sparkling eyes; for she knew by past experience, that from thenceforward, with an air of proprietary that was very provoking, he would be certain to hover constantly beside her; and now, after paying the usual compliments to the two ladies, his lordship condescended to honour me with a glance and a smile, but not with his hand.

'Ah, how do you do, Mr. Hardinge—or shall I have the pleasure of saying Captain Hardinge?' said he.

'Fortune has not so far favoured me—I am only a sub still.'

'So was Wellington in his time,' said Sir Madoc, tapping me on the shoulder.

'Ah, but you'll soon be off to the East now, I suppose.' (His eyes expressed the words, 'I hope.') 'We shall soon come to blows with those Russian fellows, and then promotions will come thick and fast. I have it as a certainty from Aberdeen himself, that a landing somewhere on the enemy's coast cannot be much longer delayed now.'

'And with one-half our army dead, and the other half worn out by camp-fever, cholera, and sufferings at Varna, we shall take the field with winter before us—a Russian winter too !' said Sir Madoc, who was a bitter opponent of the Ministry.

Ere Pottersleigh could reply, to avert any discussion of politics, the Countess spoke.

'I trust,' said she, 'that the paragraph in the *Court Journal* and other papers, which stated that your title is about to be made an earldom, is something more than mere rumour ?'

'Much more, I have the pleasure to inform you,' mumbled this hereditary legislator. 'I have already received official notice of the honour intended me by her Majesty. I supported the Aberdeen ministry so vigorously throughout this Russian affair, clearing them, so far as in me lay, from the allegations of vacillation, that in gratitude they were bound to recognise my services.'

He played with his eyeglass, and glanced at Estelle. She seemed to be looking intently at the shifting crowd; yet she heard him, for a slight colour crossed her cheek.

'So Potter is to be an earl,' thought I; 'and she perhaps is contrasting *his* promotion with that which I have to hope for.'

Even this brief conversation by its import

made me fear that my dreams might never come
to pass—that my longings were too impossible for
fulfilment. I envied Caradoc, who, having no dis-
tinction of rank to contend with in his love affair,
seemed to be getting on very well with Winifred
Lloyd, who, to his great delight, had made him
her *aide-de-camp* and useful friend during the day.

'Our troops will find it tough work encounter-
ing the Russians, I expect,' said Lord Pottersleigh;
'for although the rank and file are utter barba-
rians, Mr. Hardinge, many of their officers are
men of high culture, and all regard the Czar as a
demigod, and Russia as holy.'

'I met some of them when I was in the north
of Europe,' said Guilfoyle—who, being rather ignored by Pottersleigh, felt ruffled, if not secretly
enraged and disposed to contradict him; 'and
though I think all foreigners usually absurd—'

'Ah, that is a thoroughly English and somewhat provincial idea,' said his lordship, quietly
interrupting him; 'but I have read of an old
Carib who said, "The only obstinate savages I
have met are the English; they adopt none of our
customs."'

'To adopt their *dress* might have been difficult

in those days; but all foreigners, and especially Russians, are somewhat strange, my lord, when judged by an English standard. I can relate a curious instance of attempted peculation in a Russian official, such as would never occur with one occupying a corresponding position here. When *attaché* at the court of Catzenelnbogen, I once visited a wealthy Russian landowner, a Count Tolstoff, who lived near Riga, at a time when he was about to receive the sum of eighty thousand silver roubles from the imperial treasury, for hemp, timber, and other produce of his estate, sold for the use of the navy. Ivan Nicolaevitch, the Pulkovnich commanding the marine infantry stationed in the fortress of Dunamunde, was to pay this money; but that official informed Tolstoff verbally—he was too wary to commit anything to paper—that unless six thousand of the roubles were left in his hands, the whole might be lost by the way, as my friend's residence was in a solitary place, and the neighbourhood abounded with lawless characters.

'On Tolstoff threatening to complain to the Emperor, the Pulkovnich most unwillingly handed over the entire sum, which was delivered in great state by a praperchich, or ensign, and six soldiers; and there we thought the matter would end. But that very night, as we sat at supper, smoking our meerschaums to digest a repast of mutton with mushrooms, *compote* of almonds and stuffed carrots—carrots scooped out like pop-guns, and loaded with mincemeat—the dining-room was softly entered by six men dressed like Russian peasants, with canvas caftans and rope girdles, bark shoes and long beards, their faces covered with crape. They threatened me with instant death by the pistol if I dared to stir; and pinioning my friend to a chair, placed the barrel of another to his head, and demanded the treasure, or to be told where it was.

'Tolstoff, who was a very cool fellow, gave me a peculiar smile, and told me in French to open the lower drawer of his escritoire, and give them every kopec I found there.

'On obtaining permission from the leader, I crossed the room, and found in the drawer indicated no money, but a brace of revolver pistols. With these, which luckily were loaded and capped, I shot down two of the intruders, and the rest fled. On tearing the masks from the fallen men, we discovered them to be—whom think you? The

Pulkovnich Nicholaevitch and the praperchich of the escort! There was an awful row about the affair, as you may imagine; but in a burst of gratitude my friend gave me this valuable ring, a diamond one, which I have worn ever since.'

'God bless my soul, what a terrible story!' exclaimed Pottersleigh, regarding the ring with interest; for Guilfoyle usually selected a new audience for each of these anecdotes, by which he hoped to create an interest in himself; and certainly he seemed to do so for a time in the mind of the somewhat simple old lord, who now entered into conversation with him on the political situation, actually took his arm, and they proceeded slowly across the lawn together. I was sorry Caradoc had not overheard the new version of the ring, and wondered how many stories concerning it the proprietor had told to others, or whether he had merely a stock on hand, for chance narration. Was it vanity, art, or weakness of intellect that prompted him? Yet I have known a Scotch captain of the line, a very shrewd fellow, who was wont to tell similar stories of a ring, and, oddly enough, over and over again to the *same* audience at the mess-table.

Being rid of both now, I resolved to lose no time in taking advantage of the situation. Sir Madoc and 'mamma' were in the refreshment tent, where I hoped they were enjoying themselves; Dora was busy with a young sub from Chester—little Tom Clavell of the 19th—who evidently thought her fête was 'awfully jolly;' Caradoc had secured Winifred for one dance—she could spare him but one—and his usual soldierly swing was now reduced to suit her measure, as they whirled amid the throng on the smoothly-shorn turf.

CHAPTER XII.

LADY ESTELLE received me with a welcome smile, for at that time all around her were strangers; and I hoped—nay, felt almost certain—that pleasure to see me inspired it, for on my approach she immediately rose from her seat, joined me, and as if by tacit and silent consent, we walked onward together.

Pottersleigh's presence at Craigaderyn Court, and the rumours it revived; something cool and patronising in his manner towards me, for he had not forgotten *that* night in Park-lane; Lady Naseby's influence against me; the chances that some sudden military or political contingency might cut short my leave of absence; the certainty that ere long I should have to 'go where glory waited' me, and perhaps something less pleasant in the shape of mutilation—the wooden leg which Dora referred to—a coffinless grave in a ghastly battle trench,—all rendered my anxiety to come to an understanding with Lady Estelle irrepressible.

My secret was already known to Phil Caradoc, fully occupied though he was with his own passion for Winifred Lloyd ; and I felt piqued by the idea of being less successful than I honestly hoped he was, for Phil was the king of good fellows, and one of my best friends.

'You have seemed very *triste* to-day—looking quite as if you lived in some thoughtful world of your own,' said Lady Estelle, when she left her seat ; ' neither laughing nor dancing, scarcely even conversing, and certainly not with me. Why is this ?'

'You have declined all dancing, hence the music has lost its zest for me.'

'It is not brilliant ; besides, it is somewhat of a maypole or harvest-home accomplishment, dancing on the grass ; pretty laborious too ! And then, as Welsh airs predominate, one could scarcely waltz to the "Noble Race of Shenkin."'

'You reserve yourself for the evening, probably ?'

'Exactly. I infinitely prefer a well-waxed floor to a lawn, however well mown and rolled. But concerning your—what shall I term it—sadness?'

'Why ask me when you may divine the cause, though I dare not explain—here at least?'

After a little pause she disengaged two flowers from her bouquet, and presenting them to me with an arch and enchanting smile—for when beyond her mother's ken, she could at times be perfectly natural—she said,

'At this floral *fête champêtre*, I cannot permit you to be the only undecorated man.'

'Being in uniform, I never thought of such an ornament.'

'Wear these, then,' said she, placing them in a button-hole.

'As your gift and for your sake?'

'If you choose, do so.'

'Ah, who would not but choose?' said I, rendered quite bright and gay even by such a trifle as this. 'But, Lady Estelle, do you know what these are emblematic of?'

'In the language of the flowers, do you mean?'

'Of course; what else could he mean?' said a merry voice; and the bright face of Dora, nestled amid her golden hair, appeared, as she joined us, flushed with her dancing, and her breast palpitating with pleasure, at a time when I most cordially wished her elsewhere. 'Yes,' she continued, 'there is a pansy; that's for thought, as Ophelia says—and a rosebud; that is for affection.'

'But I don't believe in such symbolism, Dora; do you, Mr. Hardinge?'

'At this moment I do, from my soul.'

She laughed, or affected to laugh, at my earnestness; but it was not displeasing to her, and we walked slowly on. Among the multitude of strangers—to us they were so, at least—to isolate ourselves was comparatively easy now. Besides, it is extremely probable that under the eyes of so many girls she had been rather bored by the senile assiduity of her old admirer; so, avoiding the throng around the dancers, the band, and the luncheon marquee, we walked along the terraces towards the chase, accompanied by Dora, who opened a wicket in a hedge, and led us by a narrow path suddenly to the cliffs that overhung the sea. Here we were quite isolated. Even the music of the band failed to reach us; we heard only the monotonous chafing of the waves below, and the

sad cry of an occasional sea-bird, as it swooped up
or down from its eyrie. The change from the
glitter and brilliance of the crowded lawn to this
utter solitude was as sudden as it was pleasing.
In the distance towered up Great Orme's Head,
seven hundred and fifty feet in height; its
enormous masses of limestone rock abutting
against the foam, and the ruins of Pen-y-Dinas
cutting the sky-line. The vast expanse of the
Irish Sea rolled away to the northwestward, dotted
by many a distant sail; and some eighty feet below us the surf was rolling white against the
rocky base of the headland on which we stood.

'We are just over the Bod Mynach, or
"monk's dwelling,"' said Dora. 'Have you not
yet seen it, Estelle ?'

'No; I am not curious in such matters.'

'It is deemed one of the most interesting
things in North Wales, quite as much so as St.
Tudno's Cradle, or the rocking-stone on yonder
promontory. Papa is intensely vain of being its
proprietor. Gruffyd ap Madoc hid here, when he
fled from the Welsh after his desertion of Henry
III.; so it was not made yesterday. Let us go
down and rest ourselves in it.'

'Down the cliffs?' exclaimed Lady Estelle with astonishment.

'Yes—why not? There is an excellent path, with steps hewn in the rock. Harry Hardinge knows the way, I am sure.'

'As a boy I have gone there often, in search of puffins' nests; but remember that Lady Estelle—'

'Is not a Welsh girl of course,' said Dora.

'Nor a goat, like Carneydd Llewellyn,' added her friend.

'But with Mr. Hardinge's hand to assist you,' urged Dora.

'Well, let us make the essay at once, nor lose time, ere we be missed,' said the other, her mind no doubt reverting to mamma and Lord Potters-leigh.

I began to descend the path first, accepting with pleasure the office of leading Lady Estelle, who for greater security drew off a glove and placed her hand in mine, firmly and reliantly, though the path, a ladder of steps cut in the living rock, almost overhung the sea, and the descent was not without its perils. The headland was cleft in two by some throe of nature, and down this chasm poured a little stream, at the mouth of which, as in a diminutive bay, a gaily-painted pleasure-boat of Sir Madoc's, named the Winifred, was moored, and it seemed to be dancing on the waves almost beneath us.

We had barely proceeded some twenty feet down the cliff when Dora, instead of following us, exclaimed that she had dropped a bracelet on the path near the wicket, but we were to go on, and she would soon rejoin us. As she said this she disappeared, and we were thus left alone.

To linger where we stood, almost in mid-air, was not pleasant; to return to the edge of the cliff and await her there, seemed a useless task. Why should we not continue to descend, as she must soon overtake us? I could read in the proud face of Lady Estelle, as we paused on that ladder of rock, with her soft and beautiful hand in mine, that she felt in a little dilemma.

So did I, but my heart beat happily; to have her so entirely to myself, even for ten minutes, was a source of joy.

While lingering thus, I gradually led our conversation up to the point I wished, by talking of my too probable speedy departure for another land; of the happy days like the present, which I should

never forget; of herself. My lips trembled as my
heart seemed to rise to them; and forgetting the
perilous place in which we stood, and remembering only that her hand was clasped in mine, I
began to look into her face with an expression of
love and tenderness which she could not mistake;
for her gaze soon became averted, her bosom
heaved, and her colour came and went; and so,
as the minutes fled, we were all unaware that
Dora had not yet returned; that the sultry afternoon had begun to darken as heavy dun clouds
rolled up from the seaward, and the air become
filled with electricity; and that a sound alleged
to be distant thunder had been heard at Craigaderyn Court, causing some of the guests to prepare
for departure, despite Sir Madoc's assurances that
no rain would fall, as the glass had been rising.

Dora was long in returning; so long that,
instead of waiting or retracing our steps, proceeding hand in hand, and more than once Lady
Estelle having to lean on my shoulder for support,
we continued to descend the path in the face of
the cliff—a path that ultimately led us into a
terrible catastrophe.

CHAPTER XIII

A PROPOSAL.

A LONG time elapsed and we did not return ; but
amid the bustle that reigned in and around Craigaderyn Court, our absence was not observed so soon
as it might otherwise have been, the attention of
the many guests being fully occupied by each
other.

The proposal of Dora's health devolved upon
Lord Pottersleigh as the senior bachelor present,
and it was drunk amid such cheers as country
gentlemen alone can give. Then Sir Madoc, who
had a horror of after-dinner speeches in general,
replied tersely and forcibly enough, because the
words of thanks and praise for his youngest girl
came straight from his affectionate heart ; but his
white handkerchief was freely applied to the nervous task of polishing his forehead, which gave him

a sense of relief; for the worthy old gentleman was no orator, and closed his response by drinking to the health of all present in Welsh.

'Our good friend's ideas are somewhat antiquated,' said Pottersleigh to Guilfoyle, who now stuck to him pretty closely; 'but he is a thorough gentleman of an old school that is passing away.'

His lordship, however, looked the older man of the two.

'Antiquated! By Jove, I should think so,' responded the other, who instinctively disliked his host; 'ideas old as the days when people made war without powder and shot, went to sea without compasses, and pegged their clothes for lack of buttons; but he is a hospitable old file, and his wine—this Château d'Yquem, for instance, is excellent.'

Pottersleigh gave the speaker a quiet stare, and then, as if disliking this style of comment, turned to Lady Naseby for the remainder of the repast.

The overcasting of the day and a threatening of rain had put an end to much of the dancing on the flower-terrace, and of the promenading in the garden and grounds. The proposal of Dora's health had been deemed the close of the fête; the servants had begun to prepare for the ball, and many of the guests, whose invitation did not include that portion of the festivities—for the grounds, of course, would hold more than the hall—were beginning to depart, while a few still lingered in the conservatories, the library, or the picture gallery; thus, though Caradoc was looking through them for me, with a shrewd idea that I was with Lady Estelle, he could not for the life of him imagine *where;* besides, Phil was anxious to make the most of his time with Miss Lloyd.

The breaking of the guests into groups caused our absence to be long unnoticed, especially while carriages, gigs, drags, wagonnettes, and saddle-horses were brought in succession to the door; cloaks and shawls put on, ladies handed in, and the stream of vehicles went pouring down the long lime avenue and out of the park.

'You have danced but once to-day with Mr. Caradoc, he has told me,' said Dora in a low voice, as she passed her sister.

'I had so many to dance with—so many to introduce; and then, think of the evening before us.'

'He loves you quite passionately, I think, Winny dear; more than words can tell.'

' So it would seem,' replied Winifred, smiling over her fan.

' Why—how ?'

' He has never spoken to me on the subject.'

' He will do so before this evening is over, or I am no true prophetess,' said Dora, as she threw back the bright masses of her hair.

' That I don't believe.'

' Why ?'

' Because he wears at his neck a gold locket, the contents of which no one has seen; and Mr. Guilfoyle assures me that it holds the likeness of a lady.'

' Well, time will prove,' replied Dora, as she was again led away by her new admirer, the little sub from Chester; but her prediction came true.

Winifred felt instinctively that she was the chief attraction to Caradoc, and was exciting in his breast emotions to which she could not respond. Again and again, when asking her to dance, she had urged in reply, that he would please her more by dancing with others, as there were present plenty of country girls to whom a red coat was quite a magnet; so poor Caradoc found plenty of

work cut out for him.   Pressed at last by him,
Winifred said, while fanning herself,

'Do excuse me ; to-night I shall reward you
fully ; but meanwhile we may take a little promenade.   I think all who are to remain must know
each other pretty well now ;' and taking his arm
they passed from the great marquee along the now
deserted terrace, to find that the sky was so over-
cast and the wind so high, that they turned into
an alley of the conservatory, where she expected to
find some of their friends, but it was empty ; and
as Caradoc's face, and the tremulous inflections of
his voice, while he was uttering mere commonplaces about the sudden change in the weather,
the beauty of the flowers, the elegance of the conservatory, and so forth, told her what was passing
in his mind, she became perplexed, annoyed with
herself, and said hurriedly,

'Let us seek Lady Naseby ; I fear that we are
quite neglecting her—and she is somewhat particular.'

'One moment, Miss Lloyd, ere we go ; I have
so longed for an opportunity to speak with you—
alone, I mean—for a moment—even for a moment,' said he.

Winifred Lloyd knew what was coming; there was a nervous quivering of her upper lip, which was a short one, and showed a small portion of her white teeth, usually imparting an expression of innocence to her face, while its normal one was softness combined with great sweetness. Caradoc had now possessed himself of her right hand, thus without breaking away from him, and making thereby a species of 'scene' between them, an episode to be avoided, she could not withdraw, but stood looking shyly and blushingly half into his handsome face, while he spoke to her with low and broken but earnest utterances.

'I have decoyed you hither,' said he, 'and you will surely pardon me for doing so, when you think how brief is my time now, here, in this happy home of yours — even in England itself; and when I tell you how anxious I have been to —to address you—'

'Mr. Caradoc,' interrupted the girl, now blushing furiously behind her fan, 'your moments will soon become minutes!'

'Would that the minutes might become hours, and the hours, days and years, could I but spend them with you! Listen to me, Miss Lloyd—'

'Not at present—do, pray, excuse me—I wish to speak with Dora.'

But instead of having her hand released, it was now pressed by Caradoc between both of his.

'I will not detain you very long,' said he sadly, almost reproachfully; 'you know that I love you; every time my eyes have met yours, every time I have spoken, my voice must have told you that I do dearly, and if the fondest emotions of my heart—'

'A soldier's heart, of which little scraps and shreds have been left in every garrison town?'

'Do not laugh at my honest earnestness!' urged Caradoc with a deep sigh.

'Pardon me, I do not laugh; O think not that I could be guilty of such a thing!' replied Winifred, colouring deeper than ever.

Beautiful though she was, and well dowered too, this was the first proposal or declaration that had been made to her. The speaker was eminently handsome, his voice and eyes were full of passion and earnestness, and she could not hear him without a thrill of pleasure and esteem.

'I know that I am not worthy of you, perhaps; but—'

'I thank you, dear Mr. Caradoc, but—but—more is impossible.'

'Impossible—why?'

She grew quite pale, now, but he still retained her hand; and her change of colour was perhaps unseen by him, for there was little light in the conservatory, the evening clouds being dark and dense without.

'Miss Lloyd—Winifred—dearest Winifred—I love you, love you with all my heart and soul!'

'Do not say so, I implore you!' said she in an agitated voice, and turning away her head.

'Do you mean to infer that you are already engaged?'

'No.'

'Or that you love another?'

'That is not a fair question,' she replied, with a little hauteur of manner.

'It is, circumstanced as I am, and after the avowal I have made.'

'Well, I do—not.'

'And yet you cannot love me? Alas, I am most unfortunate!'

'Let this end, dear Mr. Caradoc,' said Winifred, almost sobbing, and deeply repenting that she had taken his arm for a little promenade that was to end in a proposal. Phil, being in full uniform, played with, or swung somewhat nervously, the tassels of his crimson sash, a favourite resort of young officers when in any dubiety or dilemma. After a little pause—

'May I speak to Sir Madoc on the subject?' he asked.

'No.'

'Perhaps my friend Harry Hardinge might advise—'

'Nay, for Heaven's sake don't confer with him on the matter at all!'

'Why?' said he, startled by her earnestness.

'Would you make love to me through *him*— through another?'

'You entirely mistake my meaning.'

'What *do* you mean?'

'Simply what I have said; that I love you, esteem and admire you; that you are indeed most dear to me, and that if I had the approval—'

'Of the lady whose likeness is in your locket; so treasured that a secret spring secures it?' said she, suddenly remembering Dora's words as a means of escape.

' Yes, especially with her approval. I should then be happy, indeed. I know not how you came to know of it; but shall I show you the likeness ?'

' If you choose,' said Winifred, thinking in her heart, 'Poor fellow, it must be his mother's miniature ;' but when Phil touched a spring and the locket flew open, she beheld a beautiful coloured photo of *herself*.

' Good Heavens !' she exclaimed, 'how came you by this ?'

' Hardinge had two in the barracks, and I begged one from him.'

' Hardinge—Harry Hardinge ! That was most unfair of him,' said she, her agitation increasing ; ' he is one of our oldest friends.'

' May I be permitted to keep it ?'

' O, no ; not there—not there, in a locket at your neck.'

' Be it so ; your slightest wish is law to me ; but be assured, Miss Lloyd, the heart near which it lies was never offered to woman before.'

' I can well believe you ; but—hush, here are people coming !'

Sir Madoc and Lady Naseby entered the conservatory somewhat hurriedly, followed by two or three of the guests.

'Lady Estelle! Is Lady Estelle here?' they asked simultaneously.

'No,' replied Caradoc.

'Nor Harry Hardinge?'

'We are quite alone, papa,' said Winifred, in a voice the agitation of which, at another time, must have been apparent to all; for no woman can hear a declaration of love or receive a proposal quite unconcerned, especially from a handsome young fellow who was so earnest as Philip Caradoc, around whom the coming departure for the seat of war shed a halo of melancholy interest, and who, by the artless production of the locket, proved that he had loved her for some time past, and secretly too.

'What the deuce is the meaning of this?' exclaimed Sir Madoc, with an expression of comicality, annoyance, and alarm mingling in his face; 'the servants can nowhere find her!'

'Find who?' asked Lord Pottersleigh, opening his snuff-box as he shambled forward.

'Why, Lady Estelle.'

His lordship took a pinch, paused for the re-
freshing titillation of a sneeze, and then said,

'Indeed—surprising—very!'

'And Hardinge is missing too, you say?' said
Phil. 'How odd!'

'Odd! egad, I think it *is* odd; they have not
been seen by any one for more than two hours,
and a regular storm has come on!'

Phil and Miss Lloyd had been too much occupied, or they must have remarked the bellowing
of the wind without, and the sudden darkening of
the atmosphere.

'O papa, papa!' exclaimed Dora, now rushing
in from the lawn, 'something dreadful must have
happened. I left them on the verge of the cliffs;
returning to look for the bracelet you gave me, I
met my partner, Mr. Clavell of the 19th; we began dancing again, and I forgot all about them.'

'On the cliffs!' exclaimed several voices repre-
hensibly and fearfully.

'Yes,' continued Dora, beginning to weep; 'I
took them through the park wicket, and suggested
a visit to the Bôd Mynach.'

'Suggested this to Estelle! She is not, as we
are, used to such paths and places, and you tell us

of it only now!' exclaimed Winifred, with an expression of reproach and anguish sparkling in her eyes.

'My God, an accident must have occurred! The wind—weather—compose yourself, Lady Naseby; Gwyllim, ring the house-bell, and summon every one,' cried Sir Madoc; 'not a moment is to be lost.'

'O, what is all this you tell me now, Dora?' exclaimed Winifred as she started from the conservatory, with her lips parted, her dark eyes dilated, and her hair put back by both her trembling hands.

Poor Phil Caradoc and his proposal were alike forgotten now; and he began to fear that, like Hugh Price of ours, in making love he had made some confounded mistake.

Querulous, and useless so far as searching or assisting went, Lord Pottersleigh nevertheless saw the necessity of affecting to do something, as a man, as a gentleman, and a very particular friend of the Naseby family. Accoutred in warm mufflings by his valet, with a mackintosh, goloshes, and umbrella, he left the house half an hour after every one else, and pottered about the lawn, exclaiming from time to time,

'Such weather! such a sky! ugh, ugh! what

the devil can have happened?' till a violent fit of
coughing, caused by the keen breeze from the
sea, and certain monitory twinges of gout, compelled him to return to his room and wait the
event there, making wry faces and sipping his
colchicum, while sturdy old Sir Madoc conducted
the search on horseback, galloping knee-deep
among fern, searching the vistas of the park, and
sending deer, rabbits, and hares scampering in
every direction before him.

Above the bellowing of the stormy wind, that
swept the freshly torn leaves like rain against the
walls and mullioned windows of the old house, or
down those long umbrageous vistas where ere long
the autumn spoil would be lying thick, rose and fell
the clangour of the house-bell. Servants, grooms,
gamekeepers, and gardeners were dispatched to
search, chiefly in the wild vicinity of the now
empty Bôd Mynach; but no trace could be found
of Lady Estelle or her squire, save a white-laced
handkerchief, which, while a low cry of terror escaped her, Lady Naseby recognised as belonging
to her daughter. On it were a coronet and the
initials of her name.

It had been found by Phil Caradoc with the

aid of a lantern, when searching along the weedy rocks between the silent cavern and the seething sea, which was now black with the gathered darkness and a mist from the west.

There was no ball at Craigaderyn Court that night.

CHAPTER XIV.

THE UNFORESEEN.

In this world, events unthought of and unfore-
seen are always happening; so, as I have hinted,
did it prove with me, on the epoch of Dora's
birthday fête.

It was not without considerable difficulty and
care on my side, trepidation and much of annoyance at Dora on that of Lady Estelle, mingled
with a display of courage which sprang from her
pride, that I conducted her by the hand down the
old and time-worn flight of narrow steps—which
had been hewn, ages ago, by some old Celtic hermit in the face of the cliff—till at last we stood
on the little plateau that lies between the mouth
of his abode and the sea, which was chafing and
surging there in green waves, that the wind was
cresting with snowy foam.

On our right the headland receded away into a wooded dell, that formed part of Craigaderyn Park. There a little *rhaidr* or cascade came plashing down a fissure in the limestone rocks, and fell into a pool, where a pointed pleasure-boat, named the Winifred, was moored. On our left the headland, that towered some eighty feet above us, formed part of the bluffs or sea-wall that stretched away to the eastward, and, sheer as a rampart, met the waves of the wide Irish Sea.

Before us opened the arched entrance of the monk's abode—a little cavern or cell, that had been hollowed by no mortal hand. Its echoes are alleged to be wonderful; and it has been of old used as a hiding-place in times of war and trouble, and by smugglers for storing goods, where the knights of Craigaderyn could find them without paying to the king's revenue. It has evidently been what its name imports—the chapel and abode of some forgotten recluse. A seat of stones goes round the interior, save at the entrance. A stone pillar or altar had stood in its centre. A font or stone basin is there, and from it there flows a spring of clear water, with which the follower of St. David was wont to baptise the little savages of

Britannia Secunda; and where now, in a more pleasant and prosaic age, it has supplied the tea and coffee kettles of many a joyous party, who came hither boating or fishing from Craigaderyn Court; and above that stone basin the hermit's hand has carved the somewhat unpronounceable Welsh legend:

'Heb Dduw, heb ddim.'*

'A wonderful old place! But I have seen caverns enough elsewhere, and this does not interest me. I am no archæologist,' said Lady Estelle—'besides, where is Dora?' she added, looking somewhat blankly up the ladder of steps in the cliff by which we were to return : and she speedily became much less alive to the beauty of the scenery than to a sense of danger and awkwardness in her position.

There was no appearance of Dora Lloyd, and we heard no sound in that secluded place, save the chafing of the surf, the equally monotonous pouring of the waterfall, and the voices of the sea-birds as they skimmed about us.

* Without God, without everything.

I thought that Lady Estelle leant upon my arm
a little heavier than usual, and remembered, that
when I took her hand in mine to guide her down,
she left it there firmly and confidingly.

'May I show you the grotto?' said I; and my
heart beat tumultuously while I looked in her
face, the rare beauty of which was now greatly enhanced by a flush, consequent on our descent and
the sea-breeze.

'O no, no, thanks very much; but let us return to the park ere we be missed. Give me your
hand, Mr. Hardinge. If we came down so quickly,
surely we may as quickly ascend again.'

'Shall I go first?'

'Please, do. The caves of Fingal, or Ele-
phanta and Ellora to boot, were not worth this
danger.'

'I have come here many a time for a few sea-
birds' eggs,' said I, laughing, to reassure her.

But the ascent proved somehow beyond her
power. The wind had risen fast, and was sweeping round the headland now, blowing her dress
about her ankles, and impeding her motions. She
had only ascended a little way when giddiness or
terror came over her. She lost all presence of

mind, and began to descend again. Thrice, with my assistance, she essayed to climb the winding steps that led to the summit, and then desisted. She was in tears at last. As all confidence had deserted her, I proposed to bind her eyes with a handkerchief; but she declined. I also offered, if she would permit me to leave her for a few minutes, to reach the summit, and bring assistance; but she was too terrified to remain alone on the plateau of rock, between the cell and the water.

'Good Heavens!' she exclaimed, when, like myself, perhaps she thought of Lady Naseby, 'what shall I do? And all this has been brought about by the heedless suggestions of Dora Lloyd —by her folly and impulsiveness! Will she never return to advise us?'

Nearly half an hour had elapsed, and a dread that she, that I—that both of us—must now be missed, and the cause of surmise, roused an anger and pride in her breast, that kindled her eye and affected her manner, thus effectually crushing any attempt to intrude my own secret thoughts upon her.

'What *are* we to do, Mr. Hardinge? Here we cannot stay; I dare not climb; not a boat is to be seen ; the sun has almost set, and see, how dense a mist is coming on !'

I confess that I had not observed this before, so much had I been occupied by her own presence, by her beauty, and by entreating that she would 'screw her courage to the sticking-point,' and ascend where I had seen the two pretty Lloyds trip from step to step in their mere girlhood, to the horror, certainly, of their French governess ; but knowing that a fog from the sea was rolling landward in dense masses, and that the evening would be a stormy one, I felt intense anxiety for Lady Estelle, and certainly left nothing unsaid to reassure her, firmly yet delicately—for good breeding becomes a second nature, and is not forgotten even in times of dire emergency ; then how much less so when we love, and love as I did Estelle Cressingham ?—but all my arguments were in vain.

There was in her dark eyes a wild and startled brilliance, a hectic spot on each pale cheek. Her innate pride remained, but her courage was gone. She trembled, and her breath came short and quick as she said,

'Who would have dreamt that I—*I* should

have acted thus? More heedlessly even than Dora, for she is a Welsh girl, and, like a goat, is used to such places. And now there is no aid— not even the smallest boat in sight!'

'Of what have I been thinking!' I exclaimed. 'The pleasure-boat which belongs to the grotto is moored yonder in the creek, where some visitor, who preferred the short cut up the cliff, has evidently left it. If you will permit me to place you in it, I can row across the mouth of the waterfall to the other side, where a Chinese bridge will enable us at once to reach the lawn.'

'Why did you not think of this before?' she asked, with something of angry reproach almost flashing in her eyes.

'Will you make the attempt?'

'Of course. O, would that you had thought of it before!'

'Come, then, though the wind has risen certainly; and among so many guests, our absence may have been unnoticed yet.'

I reached the boat—a gaudily painted shallop, seated for four oars. There were but two, however; these were enough; but as ill-luck would have it, she was moored to a ring-bolt in the rocks by a padlock and chain, which I had neither the strength nor the means of breaking. This was a fresh source of delay, and Lady Estelle's whole frame seemed to quiver and vibrate with impatience, while every moment she raised her eyes to the cliff, by which she expected succour or searchers to come.

What the deuce was she—were *we*—to say to all this? With a girl possessed of more nerve and firmness of mind this matter could never have taken such a turn, and the delay had never occurred. This *malheur* or mishap—this variation from the strict rules laid down by such matrons as the Countess of Naseby—looked so like a scheme, that I felt we were in a thorough scrape, and knew there was not a moment to be lost in making our appearance at the Court.

By a stone I smashed the padlock, and casting loose the boat, brought it to where Lady Estelle stood, beating the rock impatiently with her foot; and, handing her on board, seated her in the stern-sheets, but with some difficulty, as the west wind was rolling the waves with no small fury now past the headland, in which the black Bôd Mynach gaped.

'Pull with all your strength, Mr. Hardinge. Dear Mr. Hardinge, let us only be back in time, and I shall ever thank you!' she exclaimed.

'All that man can do, I shall,' was my enthusiastic reply.

I could pull a good stroke-oar, and had done so steadily in many a regimental and college boat-race and regatta; but now there ensued what I never could have calculated upon. Excited by the desire of pleasing Lady Estelle by landing her on the opposite side of the tiny bay with all speed—desirous, when seated opposite to her, face to face, of appearing to some advantage by an exhibition of strength and skill—at each successive stroke, as I shot the light boat seaward, I almost lifted it out of the water. I had to clear a rock, over which the water was foaming and gleaming in green and gold amid the sinking sunshine, ere I headed her due westward, and in doing so I cleared also the headland, which rose like a tower of rock from the sea, crowned by a clump of old elms, wherein some rooks had taken up their quarters in times long past.

'O, Mr. Hardinge,' said Lady Estelle, while grasping the gunwale with both hands, and looking up, 'how had I ever the courage to come down such a place? It looks fearful from this!'

Ere I could reply, the oar in my right hand broke in the iron rowlock with a crash. The wood had been faulty. By this mishap I lost my balance, and was nearly thrown into the sea, as the boat careered over on a wave. Thus the *other* was torn from my grasp, and swept far beyond my reach.

I was powerless now—powerless to aid either her or myself.

The tide was ebbing fast. The strong west wind, and the current running eastward, influenced by the flow of the Clwyde, and even of the Dee, ten miles distant, swept the now useless boat past the abutting headland, and along the front of those cliffs which rise like a wall of rock from the sea, and where, as the mist gathered round us, our fate would be unseen, whether we were dashed against the iron shore, or swept out into the ocean.

The red sunset was fading fast on distant Orme's Head, where myriads of sea-birds are ever revolving, like gnats in the light amid its grand and inaccessible crags. It was dying too, though tipping them with flame, on Snowdon's peaks, the eyrie of the golden eagle and the peregrine falcon, and on the smaller range of Carneydd Llewellyn. Purple darkness was gathering in the grassy vales between, and blue and denser grew those shadows as the cold gray mist came on, and the sombre glow of a stormy sunset passed away.

Soon the haze of the twilight blurred, softened, and blended land and sea to the eastward. The sharp edge of the new moon was rising from a dark and trembling horizon, whence the mist was coming faster and more fast, and the evening star, pale Hesperus, shone like a tiny lamp amid the opal tints of a sky that was turning fast to dun and darkness.

The rolling mist soon hid the star and the land too, and I only knew that we were drifting helplessly away.

CHAPTER XV

WHAT THE MOON SAW.

THE absence of the boat from its mooring-place was soon observed, and surmises were rife that we must infallibly have gone seaward.

But why? It seemed unaccountable—and at such a time too! The idea that Lady Estelle's heart should fail her in attempting to return by the cliff never occurred to any save Winifred, who knew more of her friend's temperament than the rest, and for a time, with others, the ardent and courageous girl searched the shore, and several boats were put forth into the mist; but in vain, and ere long the strength and violence of the wind drove even Sir Madoc and all his startled guests to the shelter of the house.

Muffled in silk cloaks and warm shawls or otter-skin jackets, the ladies had lingered long on

the terraces, on the lawn and avenues, while the
lights of the searchers were visible, and while
their hallooing could be heard at times from the
rocks and ravines, where they swung their lan-
terns as signals, in hopes that the lost ones might
see them.

Lord Pottersleigh snuffed and ejaculated from
time to time, and ere long had betaken himself
to his room. Caradoc, Guilfoyle — who seemed
considerably bewildered by the affair—young Clavell of the 19th, and other gentlemen, with Gwyllim the butler, Morgan Roots the gardener, Bob
Spurrit, and the whole male staff of the household,
manfully continued their search by the shore.

There the scene was wild and impressive.
Before the violence of the bellowing wind, the
mist was giving place to the pall-like masses of
dark clouds, which rolled swiftly past the pale
face of the new moon, imparting a weird-like aspect to the rocky coast, against which the sea was
foaming in white and hurrying waves, while the
sea-birds, scared alike by the shouts and the
lights of the searchers, quite as much as by the
storm, screamed and wheeled in wild flights about
their eyries.

Moments there were when Caradoc thought the search was prosecuted in the wrong direction, and that, as there had probably been an elopement, this prowling along the seashore was absurd.

'Can it be,' said he inaudibly, 'that the little boy who cried for the moon has made off with it bodily? If so, this will be rather a "swell" affair for the mess of the Royal Welsh.'

Slowly passed the time, and more anxious than all the rest—Lady Naseby of course excepted—the soft-hearted Winifred was full of dismay that any catastrophe should occur to two guests at Craigaderyn, and she listened like a startled fawn to every passing sound.

Dora, as deeming herself the authoress of the whole calamity, was completely crushed, and sat on a low stool with her head bowed on Lady Naseby's knee, sobbing bitterly ever and anon, when the storm-gusts howled among the trees of the chase, shook the oriels of the old mansion, and made the ivy leaves patter on the panes, or shuddering as she heard the knell-like ding-dong of the house-bell occasionally. The masses of her golden hair had been dishevelled by the wind

without; but she forgot all about that, as well as
about her two solemn engagements made with Tom
Clavell for the morrow; one, the mild excitement
of fishing for sticklebacks in the horse-pond, and
the other, a gallop to the Marine Parade of Llandudno, attended by old Bob Spurrit; for the little
sub of the 1st York North Riding was, *pro tem.*,
the bondsman of a girl who was at once charming
and childish, petulant and more than pretty.

Heavily and anxiously were passed the minutes, the quarters, and the hours.

Messenger after messenger to the searchers by
the shore went forth and returned. Their tidings
were all the same; nothing had been seen or
heard of the boat, of Lady Estelle, or of her companion.

Nine o'clock was struck by the great old clock
in the stable court, and then every one instinctively looked at his or her watch. Half-past nine,
ten, and even midnight, struck, without tidings
of the lost. By that time the mist had cleared
away, the tide had turned, and the west wind was
rolling the incoming sea with mightier fury on
the rock-bound shore.

The first hours of the morning passed without

intelligence, and alarm, dismay, and grief reigned supreme among the pallid group at Craigaderyn Court. All could but hope that with the coming day a revelation might come for weal or woe; and as if to involve the disappearance of the missing ones in greater mystery, if it did not point to a terrible conclusion, the lost pleasure-boat was discovered by a coastguardsman, high and dry, and bottom up, on a strip of sandy beach, some miles from Craigaderyn; but of its supposed occupants not a trace could be found, save a lace cuff, recognised as Lady Estelle's, wedged or washed into the framework of the little craft, thus linking her fate with it.

Ours was indeed a perilous situation. We were helplessly adrift on a stormy sea, off a rock-bound coast, in a tiny boat, liable to swamping at any moment, without oars or covering, the wind rising fast, while the darkness and the mist were coming down together.

I had no words to express my anxiety for what one so delicately nurtured as Estelle might suffer. My annoyance at the surmises and wonder naturally excited by our protracted absence; quizzical, it might be equivocal, inferences drawn from it—

I thought nothing of these. I was beyond all such minor considerations, and felt only solicitude for her safety, and a terror of what her fate might be. All other ideas, even love itself—though that very solicitude was born of love—were merged for the time in the tenderest anxiety.

If her situation with me was perilous, what had it been if with Lord Pottersleigh? But had she been with him, no such event as a descent to that unlucky pleasure grotto could have been thought of. Though pale and terrified, not a tear escaped her now; but her white and beautiful face was turned, with a haggard aspect, to mine.

A life-buoy happened to be in the boat, and without a word I tied it to her securely.

'Is there not one for you?' she asked piteously, laying a hand on mine.

'Think not of me, Lady Estelle; if you are saved, what care I for myself?'

'You swim, then?'

'A little, a very little; scarcely at all.'

'You are generous and noble, Mr. Hardinge! O, if kind God permits me to reach the land safely, I shall never be guilty of an act of folly like this again. Mamma says—poor mamma!—that it is birth, or blood, which carries people through great emergencies; but who could have foreseen such a calamitous contretemps as this? And who could have been a greater coward than I? I should have made a steady attempt at yonder pitiful cliff; to fail was most childish, and I have involved you in this most fatal peril.'

She sobbed as she spoke, and her eyes were full of light: but her lips were compressed, and all her soft and aristocratic loveliness seemed for a time to grow different in expression; to gather sternness, as a courage now possessed her, of which she had seemed deficient before, or it might be an obstinacy born of despair; for the light boat was swept hither and thither helplessly, by stem and stern alternately, on each successive wave; tossed upward on the crest of one watery ridge, or sunk downward between two that heaved up on each side as if to ingulf us; while the spoondrift, salt and bitter, torn from their tops, flew over us, as she clung with one hand to the gunwale of the tiny craft, and with the other to me.

That we were not being drifted landward was evident, for we could no longer hear the voices of the sea-birds among the rocks; and to be drifted seaward by ebb tide or current was only another phase of peril. The voice of Lady Estelle came in painful gasps as she said,

'O, Mr. Hardinge, Mr. Hardinge, we shall perish most miserably; we shall certainly be drowned! Mamma, my poor mamma, I shall never see her more!'

Though striving to reassure her, I was, for a time, completely bewildered by anxiety for what she must suffer by a terror of the sudden fate that might come upon her; and I was haunted by morbid visions of her, the brilliant Estelle, a drowned and sodden corpse, the sport of the waves —of myself I never thought—tossing unburied in the deep, or, it might be, cast mutilated on the shore; and she looked so beautiful and helpless as she clung to me now, clasping my right arm with all her energy, her head half reclined upon my shoulder, and the passing spray mingling with her tears upon her cheek. 'The drowning man is said to be confronted by a ghastly panorama of his whole life.' It may be so generally; but then I had only the horror of losing Estelle, whom I loved so tenderly.

We were now together and alone, so completely,

suddenly, and terribly alone, it might be for life or for death — the former short indeed, and the latter swift and sudden, if the boat upset, or we were washed out of it into the sea; and yet in that time of peril she possessed more than ever for me that wondrous and undefinable charm and allurement which every man finds in the woman he loves, and in her only.

'God spare us and help us!' she exclaimed; 'Mr. Hardinge, I am filled with unutterable fear;' and then she added, unconsciously quoting some poet, 'I find the thought of death, to one near death, most dreadful!'

'With you, Estelle, love might make it indeed a joy to die!' I exclaimed with a gush of enthusiasm and tenderness that, but for the terrible situation, had been melodramatic.

'I did not think that you loved me so,' said she after a little pause; and my arm now encircled her waist, while something of an invocation to heaven rose to my lips, and I repeated,

'Not think that I loved you! Do not be coquettishly unwilling to admit what you must know, that since that last happy night in London you have never been absent from my thoughts; and

here, Estelle, dear, dear Estelle, when menaced
by a grave amid these waters, I tell you that I
loved you from the first moment that I knew you!
Death stares us in the face, but tell me truly that
you—that you—'

'Love you in return? I do, indeed, dear
Harry!' she sobbed, and then her beloved face,
chilled and damp with tears and spray, came close
to mine.

'God bless you, O my darling, for this avowal!'
said I in a thick voice, and even the terrors of our
position could not damp the glow of my joy.

In all my waking dreams of her had Estelle
seemed beautiful ; but never so much so as now,
when I seemed on the eve of losing her for ever,
and my own life too ; when each successive wave
that rolled in inky blackness towards us might
tear her from my clasp ! How easily under some
circumstances do we learn the language of passion !
and now, while clasping her fast with one arm, as
with both of hers she clung to me, I pressed her
to my breast, and told her again and again how
fondly I loved her, while—as it were in a dream,
a portion of a nightmare—our boat, now filling
fast with water, was tossed madly to and fro.

And like a dream too, it seemed, the fact that I had her all to myself—for life or death, as it were—this brilliant creature so loved by many, so prized by all, and hitherto apparently so unattainable; she who, by a look, a glance, a smile, by a flirt of her fan, by the dropping of a glove or the gift of a flower, selected with point from her bouquet, had held my soul in thrall by all the delicious trifles that make up the sum and glory of love to the lover who is young. And where were we now?

Alone on the dark, and erelong it was the midnight, sea! Alone, and with me; I who had so long eyed her lovingly and longingly, even as Schön Rohtrant, the German king's daughter, was gazed at and loved by the handsome page, who dared not to touch or kiss her till he gathered courage one day, as the ballad tells us, when they were under a shady old oak.

'If God spares us to see her,' said Lady Estelle, 'what will mamma think of this terrible *fiasco* of ours?'

While Estelle loved me, I felt that I did not care very much for the dowager's views of the matter, especially at that precise moment. When on *terra firma* there would be sufficient time to consider them.

'And you are mine, darling?' said I tenderly.

'I am yours, Harry, and yours only.'

'Never shall I weary of hearing this admission; but the rumour of an engagement to Lord Pottersleigh?'

'Absurd! It has grown out of his dangling after me and mamma's wish, as I won't have my cousin Naseby.'

'And you do not hold yourself engaged—'

'Save to you, Harry, and you alone.'

And as her head again sank upon my shoulder, her pride and my doubts fled together; but now a half-stifled shriek escaped her, as the frail boat was nearly overturned by a larger wave than usual, which struck it on the counter.

We were drenched and chilled, so ours was indeed love-making under difficulties; and the time, even with her reclining in my arms, passed slowly. How many a prayer and invocation, all too deep for utterance, rose to my lips for her! The hours drew on. Would day never dawn? With all the sweet but now terrible companionship of love—for it was love combined with gloomy danger—this was our utmost craving.

The new moon, as she rose pale and sharp, like a silver sickle, from the Irish Sea, when the fog began to disperse, tipped for a little time with light the wave-tops as they rose or sank around us; but clouds soon enveloped her again; and when the tide turned, the sea ran inward, and broke wildly on the tremendous headlands of the coast. That our boat was not swamped seemed miraculous; but it was very buoyant, being entirely lined with cork, and had air-tight compartments under the seats.

A gray streak at the far horizon had spread across a gap of pale green, announcing that the short August night was past, and rapidly it broadened and brightened into day, while crimson and gold began to tip the wave-tops with a fiery hue, the whole ocean seeming to be mottled, as it were; and I could see the coast-line, as we were not quite a mile from it. In the distance were plainly visible the little town of Abergele, and those hills where Castell Cawr and the Cefn Ogo are, tinged with pink, as they rose above the white vapour that rolled along the shore.

The more distant mountain ranges seemed blue and purple against a sky where clouds of pearly-pink were floating.

Estelle was exhausted now.

Her pallor added to my misery. So many hours of pitiless exposure had proved too much for her strength, and with her eyes closed she lay helpless in my arms, while wave after wave was now impelling us shoreward, and, most happily it would seem, towards a point where the rocks opened and the water shoaled.

One enormous breaker, white-crested and over-arching, came rolling upon us. A gasp, a mutual cry to heaven, half-stifled by the bitter spray, and then the mighty volume of it ingulfed us and our boat. We had a momentary sense of darkness and blindness, a sound as of booming thunder mingled with the clangour of bells in our ears, and something of the feeling of being swept by an express train through a tunnel filled with water, for we were fairly under the latter; but I clung to the boat with one hand and arm, while the other went round Estelle with a death-like embrace, that prevented her from being swept or torn from me.

For some moments I knew not whether we were on the land or in the sea; but, though stunned by the shock, I acted mechanically. Then I remember becoming conscious of rising through the pale-green water, of inhaling a long breath, a gasping respiration, and of seeing the sunshine on the waves.

Another shock came, and we were flung on the flat or sloping beach, to be there left by the receding sea. Instead of in that place, had we been dashed against the impending rocks elsewhere, all had then been over with us.

I still felt that my right arm was clasped around Estelle; but she was motionless, breathless, and still; and though a terror that she was dead oppressed me, a torpor that I could not resist spread over all my faculties, and I sank into a state of perfect unconsciousness.

CHAPTER XVI.

THE SECRET ENGAGEMENT.

In making a circuit of his farm on the morning after the storm, Farmer Rhuddlan, while traversing a field that was bounded by a strip of the seashore, on which the ebbing surf still rolled heavily, was very much scared to find lying there, and to all appearance but recently cast up from the ocean, among starfish, weed, and wreck, an officer in full dress, and a lady (in what had been an elegant demi-toilette of blue silk and fine lace) fair, and most delicately white, but drenched, sodden, and to all appearance, as he thought, 'dearanwyl—drowned'—as she was quite motionless, with her beautiful dark hair all dishevelled and matted among the sand.

He knew me—in fact, he had known me since

boyhood, having caught me many a time in his orchard at Craig Eryri—and thought he recognised the lady. Moreover, he had heard of the search overnight, and lost no time in spurring his fat little cob in quest of succour. Some wondering rustics promptly came from a neighbouring barnyard, and by the time they arrived, Estelle and I had recovered consciousness, and struggled into a sitting position on some stones close by, whence we were beginning to look about us.

A benumbed sensation and total lack of power in my right arm warned me that an accident had occurred, and I endeavoured to conceal the circumstance from Estelle, but in vain; for when murmuring some thanks to God for our preservation, she suddenly lifted her face from my breast, and exclaimed,

'You cannot move this arm! You have been hurt, darling! Tell me about it—speak!'

'I think it is broken, Estelle,' said I, with a smile; for while I felt something almost of pleasure in the conviction that I had undergone this in saving her, thereby giving me a greater title to her interest and sympathy, I could not forget my short leave from Winchester, the war at hand, the regiment already abroad, and the active duties that were expected of me.

'Broken?' she repeated in a faint voice.

'My sword-arm—on the eve of marching for foreign service. Awkward, isn't it?'

'Awkward! O Harry, it is horrible! And all this has occurred through me and my childish folly!'

'One arm is at your service, dearest, still,' said I, while placing it round her, and assisting her to rise, as the kind old farmer returned with his people, joyful to find that we were living, after all, and that by assisting us he might in some degree repay Sir Madoc Lloyd a portion of that debt of gratitude which he owed to him.

After dispatching a mounted messenger to Craigaderyn with tidings of our safety, he had us at once conveyed to his farm-house at Craig Eryri, where dry clothing was given us, and a doctor summoned to attend me.

'You knew that we were missing—lost?' said I.

'Too well, sir,' replied the farmer, as he produced a brandy-bottle from an ancient oak cupboard. 'With all my lads I assisted in the search,' he continued in Welsh, as he could scarcely speak a word of English. 'A gentleman came here over night with a groom, both mounted, to spread the news of you and a lady having been lost somewhere below the Bôd Mynach.'

'A gentleman mounted — Mr. Caradoc, perhaps ?'

'Caradoc is one of ourselves,' said the farmer, his keen eyes twinkling; 'this one was a Sassenach—he Sir Madoc gave that lovely ring to, with a diamond as big as a horsebean, for winning a race at Chester.'

'O, Mr. Guilfoyle.'

'Yes, sir, that *is* his name, I believe,' replied Rhuddlan; and despite the gnawing agony of my arm I laughed outright, for the quondam German *attaché* would seem to have actually found time to relate something new about his brilliant to the simple old farmer, and while the fate of Lady Estelle was yet a mystery. As for *mine*, I shrewdly suspected he cared little about that.

Attired by the farmer's wife in the best clothing with which she could provide her, Lady Estelle, pale, wan, and exhausted, was seated near a fire to restore warmth to her chilled frame, while I retired with the medical man, who found my unlucky arm broken above the elbow; fortunately, the fracture was simple, and in no way a compound one. The bones were speedily set, splinted, and bandaged; and clad in a suit provided for me by Farmer Rhuddlan—to wit, a pair of corduroy knee-breeches, a deeply flapped double-breasted waistcoat, which, from its pattern, seemed to have been cut from a chintz bed-cover, so gorgeous were the roses and tulips it displayed, a large loose coat of coarse gray Welsh frieze, with horn buttons larger than crown pieces, each garment 'a world too wide'—I presented a figure so absurd and novel that Estelle, in spite of all the misery and danger we had undergone, laughed merrily as she held out to me in welcome a hand of marvellous form and whiteness, the hand that was to be mine in the time to come; and I seated myself by her side, while the farmer and his wife bustled about, preparing for the certain arrival of Sir Madoc and others from the Court.

'How odd it seems!' said Estelle, in a low voice, and after a long pause, as she lay back in the farmer's black-leather elbow chair, where his wife had kindly placed and pillowed her; and while she spoke, her eyes were half closed and her lips were wreathed with smiles; 'engaged to be married—and to you, Harry! I can scarcely realise it. Is this the end of all our ball-room flirtations, our Park drives, and gallops in the Row?'

'Nay, not the end of any; but a continuance of them all, I hope.'

'Scarcely ; people don't flirt after marriage— together, at least. But it will be the end of all mamma's grand schemes for me. She always hoped I should twine strawberry leaves with my marriage wreath. Heavens, how nearly I was having a wreath of seaweed !' she added with a shudder and a little gasping laugh as I kissed her hand. 'O, my poor Harry, with an arm broken, and by my means ! I shall never forgive myself—never.'

'Better an arm than if my heart had been broken by your means, Estelle,' said I in a low voice. After a little she said calmly and in an earnest tone, while her colour came and went more than once,

'We must be *secret*, secret as we are sincere; and yet such a system is repugnant to me, and to my pride of heart.'

'Secret, Estelle !' (How delicious to call her simply Estelle !) 'Why ?'

'It is most necessary—yet awhile, at least.'

'Your mamma's objections?'

'More than that.'

'What—more?'

'By papa's will mamma has entire control over all her fortune and mine too, and should I marry without her full approbation and consent, she may bequeath both if she pleases to my cousin Naseby, leaving but a pittance to me.'

'But what will not one undergo for love?' said I, gazing tenderly into her eyes.

She smiled sadly, but made no response; perhaps she thought of what love might have of luxury on a subaltern's pay and his 'expectations.'

'Fear not, Estelle,' said I, 'for your sake our engagement shall be a secret one.'

All my doubts and fears had already given place to the confidence of avowed and reciprocated affection, and in the security of that I was blindly happy. How my heart had been wont to throb when I used mentally to imagine the last interview I should have with her ere going forth to the East, with the story of my love untold; leaving her in ignorance, or partially so, of the sweet but subtle link that bound my existence to hers!

Now, the love was told; the link had become a tie, and pain of the anticipated parting became all the more keen apparently, and I prospectively reckoned one by one the weeks, the days, yea, almost the hours I might yet spend in the society of Estelle.

I was not much given to day-dreams or illusions, but, I asked of myself, was not all this most strange if I was not dreaming now? Could it be that, within a few hours—a time so short—Estelle and I had braved such peril together, and that I had achieved her plight, her troth; the promise of her hand; the acknowledgment of her love, and that all was fulfilled; the coveted and dearest object of my secret thoughts and tenderest wishes!

Whether our engagement was secret or not mattered little to me now. Assured of her regard, I felt in her presence and society all that calm delight and sense of repose which were so pleasing after my late tumult of anxiety, pique, jealousy, and uncertainty.

By chance or some intuition the farmer and his wife left us for a time alone, while waiting the arrival of our friends; and never while life lasts shall I forget the joy of that calm morning spent alone with Estelle in Rhuddlan's quaint little drawing-room, the windows of which faced the green Denbigh hills, on which the warm August sun shone cheerily; and often did the memory of it come back to me when I was far away, when I was shivering amid the misery of the half-frozen trenches before Sebastopol, or relieving the out pickets, when Inkermann lights were waxing pale and dim as dawn stole over those snow-clad wastes, where so thick lay the graves of men and horses, while the eternal boom and flash went on without ceasing from the Russian bastions and the allied batteries.

I felt as if I had gained life anew, and with it Estelle Cressingham. Great, indeed, was the revulsion of feeling after such peril undergone; after a night of such horror and suffering, to sit by her side, to hang over her, inspired to the full by that emotion of tenderness and rapture which no man can feel but once in life, when the first woman he has really loved admits that he has not done so in vain.

I placed on her finger—*the* engaged finger — an emerald-and-diamond ring that I valued highly, as it had once been my mother's, and in its place took one of hers, a single pearl set in blue-and-gold enamel.

The once proud beauty seemed so humble, gentle, and loving now, as she reclined with her head on my shoulder, and looked at me from time to time with a sweet quiet smile in the soft depths of her dark eyes. I forgot that she was an earl's daughter, with a noble dowry and an ambitious mother, and that I was but a sub of the Royal Welsh, with little more than his pay. I forgot that the route for Varna hung over my head like the sword of Damocles; that a separation, certain and inevitable, was hourly drawing closer and closer, though the accident which had occurred might protract it a little now.

Estelle Cressingham was a grand creature, certainly. She naturally seemed to adopt statuesque positions, and thus every movement, however careless and unstudied, was full of artistic grace. Even the misshapen garments of Mrs. Evan Rhuddlan could not quite disfigure her. The turn of her head was stately, and at times her glance, quick and flashing, had a pride in it that she was quite unconscious of. She was, as Caradoc had said, 'decidedly a splendid woman—

young lady, rather—but of the magnificent order.'
But there were tender and womanly touches, a
gentler nature, in the character of Estelle, that
lay under the artificial strata of that cumbrous
society in which she had been reared. She had
many pets at home in London and at Walcot
Park—birds and dogs, which she fed with her
own hands, and little children, who were her pen-
sioners; and if her nose seemed a proud one,
with an aristocratic curve of nostril, her short upper lip would quiver occasionally when she heard
a tale of sorrow or cruelty.

And now, from our mutual daydream, we were
roused by the sound of wheels, of hoofs, and
several voices, as some of our friends from the
Court arrived.

CHAPTER XVII.

WHAT FOLLOWED IT.

To expatiate upon the joy of all when we found ourselves safe in Craigaderyn Court again were a needless task.

Lady Estelle was conveyed at once to her own room, and placed in charge of Mademoiselle Pompon. For two entire days I saw nothing of her, and could but hover on the terrace which her windows overlooked, in the hope of seeing her; but the same doctor who came daily to dress my arm had to attend her, as she was weak, feverish, and rather hysterical after all she had undergone; while I, with my broken limb, found myself somewhat of a hero in our little circle.

' This adventure of yours will make the Bôd Mynach the eighth wonder of Wales, if it gets into print,' said Sir Madoc.

This chance was Lady Naseby's fear. She was 'full of annoyance and perplexity,' as she said, 'lest some of those busybodies who write for the ephemeral columns of the daily press should hear of the affair, and ventilate it in some manner that was garbled, sensational, and, what was worse than either, unpunishable.'

She thanked me with great courtesy, but without cordiality, for having saved her daughter's life at the expense of a broken limb, as it was by sheer strength that I prevented Estelle being torn from the boat and me. Her ladyship, however, soon dismissed the subject, and now Tiny, the snappish white shock which for some hours had been forgotten and shamefully neglected, came in for as many caresses as her daughter, if not more.

Anxious, for many obvious reasons, to gain the esteem of this cold and unapproachable dowager—even to love her, for her daughter's sake, most unlovable though she was—I was ever assiduous in my attentions; and these seemed to excite quietly the ridicule of Winifred Lloyd, while Dora said that she believed Lady Estelle must have quarrelled with me, and that I had transferred my affections to her mamma.

But little Dora saw and knew more than I supposed. On the second day after the affair, when she came with her light tripping step down the perron of the mansion, and joined me on the terrace, where I was idling with a cigar, I said,

'By the bye, why *did* you leave us, Dora, in that remarkable manner, and not return?'

'Mr. Clavell overtook me, and insisted upon my keeping an engagement to him. Moreover,' she added waggishly, 'under my music-master I have learned, that many a delightful duet becomes most discordant when attempted as a trio.'

'And for that reason you left us?'

'Precisely,' replied the lively girl, as she removed her hat, and permitted the wealth of her golden hair to float out on the wind. 'Save for your poor arm being broken, and the terrible risks you ran, I might laugh at the whole affair; for it was quite romantic—like something out of a play or novel; but it quite put an end to the ball.'

'And now that Tom Clavell has gone back to his dépôt at Chester, you can scarcely forgive me?'

'I saw that you were dying to be alone with Lady Estelle,' she retorted, 'and *now* don't you thank me?'

I certainly felt a gratitude I did not express, but doubted whether her elder sister would have approved of Dora's complicity in the matter; and affecting to misunderstand her, I said,

'Why thank you now?'

'Because,' said Dora, looking at me, with her blue eyes half closed, 'if on the top of a mountain an acquaintance ripens fast, good heavens, how must it have been with you two at the bottom of the sea!'

And she laughed merrily at her own conceit, while swinging her hat to and fro by its ribbons.

Lord Pottersleigh shook his head as if he disliked the whole affair, and nervously scanned the daily papers with spectacles on his thin aquiline nose, in expectation of seeing some absurd, perhaps impertinent, paragraph about it; and such was the old man's aristocratic vanity, that I verily believe, had he seen such, he would there and then have relinquished all his expectations—for he undoubtedly had them—of making Estelle Lady Pottersleigh, and the partner of his higher honours that were to come.

'Lady Naseby owes you a debt of gratitude, Mr. Hardinge, for saving the life of her daughter

—and I too,' he added, ' owe you an everlasting debt of gratitude.'

'You, my lord?' said I, turning round in the library, where we happened to be alone.

'Yes; for in saving her you saved one in whom I have the deepest interest. So, my dear Mr. Hardinge,' he continued pompously, looking up from the *Times*, ' if I can do aught for you at the Horse Guards, command me, my young friend, command me.'

'Thanks, my lord,' said I curtly; for his tone of patronage, and the cause thereof, were distasteful to me.

'You have of course heard the rumour of—of an engagement?'

'With Lady Estelle Cressingham?'

'Exactly,' said he, laughing till he brought on a fit of coughing—'exactly—ha, ha—ugh, ugh! How the deuce these things ooze out at clubs and in society, I cannot conceive; for even the world of London seems like a village in that way. Ah, nowhere out of our aristocracy could a man find such a wife as Lady Estelle!'

'I quite agree with you; but there is a point beyond that.'

'Indeed! what may that be?'

'To get her!' said I defiantly, enraged by the old man's cool presumption.

Was this reference to 'a rumour' merely his senile vanity, or had Estelle ignored something that really existed?

Caradoc's congratulations, though I carefully kept my own counsel, were as warm in reality as those of Guilfoyle were in pretence.

'Wish you every joy,' said the latter in a low tone, as we met in the billiard-room, where he was practising strokes with Sir Madoc.

'I don't quite understand.'

'You hold the winning-cards now, I think,' said he, with a cold glare in his eye.

'Sir?'

'I congratulate you on escaping so many perils with the Lady Estelle, and being thereby a winner.'

I had just left Pottersleigh, and was not disposed to endure much from Guilfoyle.

'The winner of what?' I asked.

'The future esteem of the Countess,' he sneered.

'Perhaps she will present me with a diamond

ring on the head of it,' said I, turning on my heel,
while Sir Madoc laughed at the hit; but whatever
he felt, Guilfoyle cloaked it pretty well by laughing, and, as a Parthian shot, quoting, with some
point, and with unruffled exterior, a line or two
from the fourth book of the *Æneid*, concerning the
storm which drew Dido and her hero into the cave.

The bearing of Winifred Lloyd now became
somewhat of a riddle to me; and on the morning
of the third day, when we all met at the breakfast
table (which was littered by cards and notes of
congratulation), and when Lady Estelle appeared,
looking so pale and beautiful, declining Mademoiselle Babette's cosmetics and pearl-powder
alike, in the loveliest morning-dress that Swan
and Edgar could produce, I was conscious that
she watched us with an interest that seemed wistful, tearful, and earnest. Whether I had a tell-
tale face, I know not. Nothing, however, could
be gathered from that of Estelle, or her mode of
greeting me and inquiring about the progress of
my broken arm towards recovery. My ring was
on her finger; but as she wore several, it passed
unnoticed, and even Dora's quick eye failed to
detect it.

Winifred had become very taciturn; and when I asked her to drive with me in the open carriage— as for a time I could not ride—she declined rather curtly, and with something of petulance, even disdain, in her tone. She never had the usual inquiries made by others concerning my fracture, nor joined with Dora in the playful rivalry of the ladies cutting for me, if no servant was near; for at table I was of course helpless. She smiled seldom, but laughed frequently; and yet it struck me there was something unwonted in the ring of her laughter, as if it came not from her heart.

The girl had a secret sorrow evidently. Was Master Phil Caradoc at the bottom of this? If not, who then? I watched her from time to time, and observed that once, when our eyes met, she seemed confused, and coloured perceptibly.

'Surely,' thought I, 'she is not resenting my half-flirtation with her the other day, when we visited her pet goat!'

She was restless, absent, listlessly indifferent, and occasionally preoccupied in manner; and in vain did I say to her more than once,

'Miss Lloyd—Winifred—what troubles you? what has vexed you?'

'Nothing troubles me, Mr. Hardinge.'

' Mr. ?'

' Well, then, Harry—and nothing vexes me.
What leads you to think so ?'

Her full-fringed dark eyes looked clearly into
mine ; they seemed moist, yet defiant, and she
tossed her pretty little head wilfully and petulantly.
I felt that I had in some way displeased her ; but
dared not press the matter, for, with all her softness of heart, she had a little Welsh temper of her
own.

Phil Caradoc gave me his entire confidence,
especially after dinner, when men become full of
talk, and inspired by bland and generous impulses.
He related, without reserve, the whole episode that
occurred in the conservatory ; and I felt some
compunction or annoyance that circumstances prevented me from having the same frankness with
him, for none would have rejoiced in my success
more warmly than he.

' For the life of me, Harry, I can't make out
what Miss Lloyd means,' said Phil, in a low voice,
as he made his Cliquot effervesce, by stirring it
with a macaroon ; ' she was ready enough to love
me as a friend, and all that sort of thing.'

' You have asked her, then ?'

' Pointedly—hardly know what I said, though —one feels so deuced queer when making love— in earnest, I mean.'

' A man can do no more than ask.'

' Except asking again ; but tell me, old fellow, have I a chance ?'

' How should I know, Phil ? But I think that the pattern sub of the Royal Welsh Fusileers, made up, like Don Juan,

" By love, by youth, and by an army tailor,"

should have a particularly good chance.'

' *You* can afford to laugh at me, Harry.'

' Far from it, Phil ; I haven't such a thought, believe me.'

' Seeing how friendly you are with these girls —with her especially—I thought you might know this. Is any other fellow spooney upon Miss Lloyd ?'

' A good many may well be ; she is lovely.'

' Well, does any one stand in her good graces ?'

' Can't say, indeed, Caradoc,' said I, as my thoughts reverted to that episode at the goat's-house, and others not dissimilar, with some emotions of compunction, as I looked into Phil's honest brown eyes.

He fancied that Winifred avoided him. In that idea he erred. She admired and loved him as a friend — a gentleman who had done her great honour; but she never thought of analysing his emotions farther than to wish him well, and to wish him away from Craigaderyn, after that scene in the conservatory; and remembering it in all its points, she was careful not to trust herself alone with him, lest the subject might be renewed; and yet she found the necessity of approaching it one day, when a sudden recollection struck her, as they were riding home together, and had cantered a little way in advance of their party.

'Now that I think of it, Mr. Caradoc,' said she, 'you must give me that likeness which you wear. I really cannot permit you to keep it, even in jest.'

'Jest!' repeated Phil, sadly and reproachfully; 'do you think so meanly of me, as to imagine that I would jest with you, or with it?'

'But I can see no reason why you should retain it.'

' Perhaps there is none—and yet, there is. It is the face of one I shall never, never forget; and it is a memento of happy days spent with you—a memento that other eyes than mine shall never look upon.'

'Do not speak thus, Mr. Caradoc, I implore you !' said Winifred, looking down on her horse's mane.

' You will permit me to keep it ?'

' For a time,' said she, trying to smile, but her lips quivered.

' Thank you, dear Winifred.'

' If shown to none.'

' While I live none shall see it; and if I die in action—as many shall surely do, and why not I as well as happier fellows ?—it will be heard of no more !'

Caradoc's voice became quite tremulous, either because of Miss Lloyd's obduracy, or that he felt, as many people do, rather pathetic at the thought of his own demise. He had already possessed himself of her whip-hand, when her horse began to rear, and in a minute more they were in the lime avenue; and this proved the last opportunity he had of reasoning with her on the subject that was nearest his heart. He now wished that he had never met Winifred Lloyd, or that, having met, and learned to love her—oddly enough, when his passion was not returned—he could be what her *ideal* was. 'In what,' thought he, 'am I wanting? Am I too rough, too soldierly, too blunt, unwinning, or what?' It was none of these; for Caradoc was a well-mannered, courteous, gentle, and pleasing young fellow, and by women unanimously deemed handsome and *distingué*. All that day he was unusually cast down and taciturn, though he strove to take an interest in the conversation around him.

'By Jove, Hardinge,' said he, 'I wish you had never brought me here, to renew the hopes I had begun to entertain in London.'

'Don't lose heart yet, Phil,' said I.

'But I have to leave for the seat of war — leave her to the chance of being loved by others, without even a promise—'

'To what troubles we are exposed in life!' said I sententiously, and feeling perhaps selfishly secure in my own affair.

'Greater troubles perhaps in death,' added Phil gloomily, as he gnawed his moustache. 'I sometimes wonder whether man was made for the world, or the world was made for man.'

'In what respect?' said I, surprised by the train of thought so unusual in him.

'Look at a newly-born infant, and you will find it difficult to determine. "He begins his life," as Pliny says, "in punishment, and only for being born."'

'Come, Phil,' said I, 'don't get into the blues; and as for Pliny, I left him with Euclid, Straith's *Fortification*, and gunnery, at Sandhurst.'

The morning mail brought letters from the dépôt-adjutant to Phil and me. Their official aspect, as Owen Gwyllim laid them on the breakfast table, attracted the attention of all. The eyes of Winifred were on me, and mine turned instinctively and sadly to Lady Estelle, who grew ashy pale, but seemed intent on some letters of her own. The adjutant's epistles were brief.

Caradoc was requested to join at once, his short leave being cancelled, as he had to go with a draft of eighty rank-and-file for the East.

My leave was extended for a fortnight, in consequence of a medical certificate received concerning the accident that had befallen me.

So that night saw poor good-hearted Phil depart; and the memory of his thick brown hair and handsome brown moustache, his clear hazel eyes and honest English face, dwelt not in the thoughts of her with whom he had left his heart behind.

He had the regimental goat in his custody; and when Winifred caressed and kissed her pet, ere it was lifted into the vehicle that was to convey it to Chester, Phil eyed her wistfully; and I knew that he would have given the best of his heart's blood to have felt but one of those kisses on his nut-brown cheek!

CHAPTER XVIII.

GUILFOYLE.

My Lord Pottersleigh and the adventurer Hawkesby Guilfoyle—for an artful, presumptuous, and very singular adventurer he eventually proved to be—could not detect that there was a secret understanding, and still less that there was any engagement, between Lady Estelle and me ; yet both were sharp enough to fancy that there was something wrong so far as they were concerned—something understood by us which to them was incomprehensible ; and the latter now referred in vain to Baden, Berlin, Catzenelnbogen, and other places where they had met so pleasantly on the Continent.

Engaged solemnly and tenderly to Estelle, I had yet the absurd annoyance of beholding Pottersleigh, who was assured of her mother's countenance

and favour (though he would have been a more
seemly suitor for herself), and whose years and
position gave him perfect confidence, hovering or
shambling perpetually about her, absorbing her
time if not her attention, mumbling his over-
strained compliments into her unwilling ear, touching her hand or tapered arm, and even patting her
lovely white shoulders from time to time with his
withered paws, and every way giving himself such
fatherly and loverlike airs of proprietary oddly
mingled, that I could with pleasure have punched
his aristocratic old head.

We frequently laughed at all this even when he
was present; for by a glance rather than a word,
Estelle could convey to me all she thought and
felt. There was something delightful in this secret
understanding, this secret community of thought
and interest, with one so young and beautiful—
more than all, when blended with it was the charm
of the most perfect success in a first affair of love;
and I thought myself one of the happiest fellows
in the world.

Superb as her toilettes were at all times, she
seemed to make little Babette Pompon take extra
pains with them now, and I felt delighted accord-

ingly, for such infinite care seemed to express a desire to please me.

Our next departure from the Court was Mr. Hawkesby Guilfoyle, whom Sir Madoc and all his visitors had begun to view with a coolness and disfavour of which the party in question found it convenient to seem quite oblivious; but it reached its culminating point through a very small matter.

One day after luncheon we had gone so far as Penmaen Mawr. The four ladies were in the open carriage; I occupied the rumble; Sir Madoc, Lord Pottersleigh, and Guilfoyle were mounted, and we were all enjoying to the fullest extent that glorious combination of marine and mountain scenery peculiar to the Welsh coast; the air was full of ozone and the sky was full of sunshine. We were all happy, and even Winifred seemed in unusually high spirits; as for Dora, she was never otherwise. The well-hung carriage rolled pleasantly along, between the beautiful green hills, past quiet villages and ancient churches, vast yawning slate quarries, green mounds and gray stones that marked where battles had been, with occasional glimpses of the Irish Sea, that stretched away to the dim horizon like a sheet of glittering glass. Estelle, by arrangement, sat with her back to the horses, so that she and I could freely converse with our eyes from time to time, under the shade of her skilfully managed parasol.

Sir Madoc on this day was peculiarly enthusiastic, and having mounted what the girls called his 'Welsh hobby,' was disposed to give it full rein.

We halted in a little sequestered glen, a lovely spot embosomed among trees, on the southern slope of the hill. The horses were unbitted; Owen Gwyllim had put the champagne bottles to cool in a runnel, where their long gilded necks and swollen corks stood invitingly up amid the rich green grass, that almost hid the murmuring water.

We had come by Caerhun, through an old and little frequented road, where Sir Madoc insisted on pointing out to us all, the many erect old battle-stones by the wayside; for his mind was now full of quaint stories, and the memory of heroes with barbarous names. Thus when Owen uncorked the Cliquot, he drank more than one guttural Welsh toast, and told us how, often in his boyhood, the road had been obstructed for

weeks by masses of rock that fell thundering from
the mountain above; and in his love of the olden
time or detestation of change, I believe he would
have preferred such barriers to progress still,
rather than have seen the lines of road and rail
that now sweep between the mountain and the sea
on the way to Holyhead.

'It was in this dell or *glyn*,' said Sir Madoc,
as he seated his sturdy figure on the grass, though
the ladies did not leave the carriage, 'that Llewellyn ap Jorwerth took prisoner the luckless William
de Breas, whom he hanged at Aber, in the time of
Henry III.'

'Why did he hang him?' asked Guilfoyle,
holding his glass for Owen to refill it.

' Because he was a handsome fellow, and found
too much favour in the eyes of his princess, whom
he dragged to the window that she might see his
body hanging lifeless on the gibbet.'

'Deuced hard lines,' said Guilfoyle, laughing.
'I thought he might have been hung because
he hadn't a pedigree, or some other enormity in
Welsh eyes.' As Sir Madoc looked at the speaker
his eyes sparkled, for the remark was a singularly
gratuitous one.

'You English,' said he, 'laugh at what you are pleased to consider our little weakness in that respect; and yet the best names in the peerage are apt to be deduced from some corporal or sergeant of William's Norman rabble.'

'Heavens, papa! when I change my name of Lloyd, I hope it won't be for that of Mrs. John Smith or Robinson!' said Dora merrily, as she heard that Sir Madoc's tone was sharp.

'Well, but you must admit that these fortuitous circumstances are deemed of small account now; for as Dick Cypher sings,

"A peer and a 'prentice now dress much the same,
    And you can't tell the difference excepting by name." '

'I don't know who your friend Dick Cypher may be,' replied Sir Madoc quietly, though evidently greatly ruffled, 'but Burke and Debrett record as ancient, names we deem but those of yesterday, and when compared with ours are as the stunted gorsebush to pine or oak—yes, sir! or as the donkey that crops thistles by the wayside when compared to the Arab horse!'

'God bless my soul!' exclaimed Pottersleigh, letting his hat sink farther on the nape of his neck, as he placed his gold glasses on his long thin nose and gazed at Sir Madoc, who tossed an empty bottle into the runnel, and continued :

'In Wales we have the lines of Kynaston, who descend from Rhodric Mawr, King of all Wales, and the daughter and co-heir of the Bloody Wolf; the Mostyns, from the Lord of Abergeleu who founded the eighth noble tribe; the Vaughans, who come from that King Rhodric who married the daughter of Meuric ap Dyfnwall ap Arthur ap Sitsylt, though that was only in the year 800; and we have the Lloyds—'

'O, papa,' exclaimed Winifred, seeing that Estelle was laughing heartily, 'we cannot listen to more; and I am sure that your muster-roll of terrible names must have quite convinced Mr. Guilfoyle of his error.'

'If it ever existed—I did but jest,' said he, bowing and smiling as he turned to her.

Sir Madoc's gust of patriotic ire passed away at the sound of his daughter's voice; but from that moment his manner to Guilfoyle underwent a marked change, for he had already more than once contrived to wound him on this his most tender point. So the usually suave and kind old

man became very cool to him as they rode home-
ward; and early that evening Guilfoyle retired to
his room, alleging that he had to write letters.

After dinner, as we idled for a little time in
the smoking-room prior to joining the ladies, Lord
Pottersleigh led the conversation gradually back
to our evening excursion, and with some hesitation
began to speak of Guilfoyle.

'You will pardon me, my dear Sir Madoc, for
venturing to speak slightingly of any friend of
yours; but—'

'Mr. Guilfoyle is no friend of mine,' said the
other hastily; 'he dropped among us from the
clouds, as it were.   When with Lady Naseby I met
him on the beach at Llandudno, he had done her
some service on the Continent, at Catzeneln—
what's-it's-name?—I invited him on the strength
of their past acquaintance—that's all.'

'Then, briefly, get rid of him, if you can.'

'What do *you* say, Harry?'

'I say with Lord Pottersleigh.'

Sir Madoc fidgeted, for his Welsh ideas of
hospitality were somewhat shocked by the idea of
'getting rid' of a guest.

'I assure you, Sir Madoc,' resumed the peer,

'that he is quite out of his place amongst us, quite; and despite his usually assumed suavity, —for it is assumed,—he lacks intensely *l'odeur de la bonne société*, though he affects it; and I overheard two of your late guests making some very dubious remarks concerning him.'

'The deuce you did!' exclaimed Sir Madoc, tossing away his half-smoked cigar.

'They spoke quite audibly, as if they cared not who might hear them.'

'Who were they?'

'Officers of the 19th, from Chester. "Guilfoyle!" I heard that fast boy Clavell exclaim, as if with surprise, to another; "is that fellow, who—" "The very same." "Then how comes he to be a guest here?" "Just what I was asking of myself, as he is tabooed everywhere. You know they say—" "*They*—who?" "O, that ubiquitous and irresponsible party so difficult to grapple with—that though he was attaché at some German place, he has been in several conspiracies to pigeon young muffs just come of age. There was particularly one poor fellow of ours whom he rooked at Hamburg of every sixpence, and who was afterwards found drowned in the Alster. And lately I

have heard that he was proprietor, or part proprietor, of a gaming-hell in Berlin." "By Jove!"
exclaimed little Clavell; "but can all this be
proved?" "No." "Why?" "He lays his plans
too deeply and surely." Then they walked towards
the marquee, and I thought I had heard enough
—quite,' added his lordship, snuffing.

Long before Pottersleigh was done, Sir Madoc
had blushed purple with stifled rage and mortification.   He said,

'My lord, you should have mentioned all this
instantly.'

'Truth is, I knew not how to approach the
subject.'

'And I have introduced this fellow to my
daughters, to my friends, and to Craigaderyn!
D—n me, I shall choke!' he exclaimed as he
started from his chair. 'He is deep as Llyn
Tegid! I have already lost considerable sums to
him at billiards, and I always thought his success
at cards miraculous.   But an end shall be put to
this instantly!—Owen! Owen Gwyllim!'

He kicked a spittoon to the other end of the
room, rang the bell furiously for the butler, and
dashed off a note to Mr. Guilfoyle.   It was suf-

ficiently curt and pointed. He expressed 'regret that a gun would not be at his service on the coming 1st of September; but that the carriage would await his orders, for Chester or elsewhere.'

Guilfoyle had doubtless been accustomed to meet with affronts such as this. Desiring his baggage to be sent after him, he departed that night with his two horses, his groom (and diamond ring); but, prior to doing so, he had the effrontery to leave P.P.C. cards for Lady Naseby and Estelle, saying that 'he should not forget their kind invitation to Walcot Park;' and rode off, scheming vengeance on me, to whom he evidently attributed the whole matter, as he informed Owen Gwyllim that he 'would yet repay me, through his solicitor, perhaps, for the interest I had taken in his affairs.'

This threw a temporary cloud over our little party, and good Sir Madoc felt a kind of sorrow for Guilfoyle as he surmised how little money he might have in his purse, forgetting that he was proprietor of a pair of horses.

To prevent her *amour propre* being wounded, we most unfortunately did not reveal this man's real character to Lady Naseby; thus, to Sir Madoc's hot temper was attributed his sudden departure.

Though Lady Estelle was excessively provoked that, through her and her mother, whom his service on the Continent had prejudiced in his favour, and through his alleged acquaintance with me, he had become Sir Madoc's guest, in a day or two the whole *contretemps* was forgotten ; but I was fated not to have seen or heard the last of Mr. Hawkesby Guilfoyle.

CHAPTER XIX.

TWO LOVES FOR ONE HEART.

By the peculiarity of our position kept much apart, or seldom finding opportunities, even in a house like Craigaderyn Court, for being alone, as it was perpetually thronged by visitors, we had to content ourselves with the joy of stolen glances that lit up the eye with an expression we alone could read, or that was understood by ourselves only; by tender touches of the hand that thrilled to the heart; and by inflections of the voice, which, do as we might, would at times become soft and tremulous. Our life was now full of petty stratagems and pretty lover-like enigmas, especially when in the presence of Lady Naseby; and now I also became afraid of Winifred Lloyd, who, unoccupied, so far as I could see, by any love-affair of her own, was almost certain, I thought, to see through mine. 'There is no conquest without the affections,' said Ninon de l'Enclos; 'and what mole is so blind as a woman in love?' Yet Estelle was careful to a degree in her bearing, and never permitted her fondness of me to lull her into a sense of security from observation.

I learned, however, from my ally Dora, that Lady Naseby was so provoked by what Estelle not inaptly termed our 'late *fiasco*,' that, save for the weight such a proceeding might have given it, they and the Viscount too would have quitted Craigaderyn Court. So they remained; but, thought I, what right had *he* to be concerned in the matter? And unless I greatly erred, I felt certain that the Countess cared not how soon I received my marching orders for that fatal shore where so many of us were to leave our bones.

Yet many a stolen kiss and snatched caress or pressure of the hand, many a whispered assurance of love, made Estelle and me supremely happy, while the few days that remained of my leave glided quickly—ah, too quickly!—past; and all desire for 'glory' apart, I was not sorry when I saw that my fractured arm would prevent my being sent with the next draft, and cause my retention for a little time longer in England. 'They who love must drink deeply of the cup of trembling,' says some one; 'for at times there will arise in their hearts a nameless terror, a sickening anxiety for the future, whose brightness all depends upon this one cherished treasure, which often proves a foreboding of some real anguish looming in the distant hours.'

As yet no forebodings came to mar my happiness; it was without alloy, save the prospect of a certain and, as we trusted to Providence, a temporary separation; yet it was well that I saw not the future, or what those distant hours had in store for me.

'Estelle,' said I, one day when a happy chance threw us together for a few minutes in an arbour of the garden, where we sometimes met at a certain hour, and separated after by different paths, like a pair of conspirators, 'when shall a period be put to all this mystery—this painful, though joyous, false position in which we find ourselves?'

'We can but wait and hope, Harry—wait and hope!' said she, while her head drooped on my shoulder, and my arm went round her.

'Wait and hope, dearest, for what ?   My promotion ?'

'That would bring the end no nearer,' said she, with a sad sickly smile.

'No, certainly ; even to be colonel of the Royal Welsh instead of a mere sub would not enhance my value much in Lady Naseby's estimation,' said I, with some bitterness. 'For what then, darling ?'

'Some change in mamma's views regarding me.'

'She will never change !'

'You know, Harry, that were you rich, I might marry you now—yes, and go to Turkey with you too!' said she, with a brightness in her eyes.

'Would to Heaven, then, that I were rich ! But being poor—'

'It is impossible.'

And we both sighed heavily.

'I am under orders for the East, and *must* take my turn of duty there, risking all the chances of war, ere I can think of home or marriage, Estelle; but when we part, if I am not to write to you, how shall I ever know that you think of me ? how hear of your health and welfare ? that you remain true to me—'

'O, doubt not that.'

'Nor do I; but it would be so sweet to see your writing, and imagine your voice reiterating the troth you plighted to me in that terrible time.'

'I shall write to you, dear, dear Harry, for I can do that freely and openly; but of you, alas! alas! I can only hear through our friends at the Court here, for you can neither write to me in London nor at Walcot Park.'

'May I not ask Miss Lloyd to receive enclosures for you? I shall be writing to her, and we are such old friends that she would think nothing of it.'

'Too old friends, I fear,' said she with a half-smiling but pointed glance; 'but for Heaven's sake think not of that. She would never consent, nor should I wish her to do so. I can of course receive what letters I choose; but servants will pry, and consider what certain coats of arms, monograms, and postal marks mean; so my Crimean correspondent would be shrewdly suspected, and myself subjected to much annoyance by mamma and her views.'

'Her *views!* This is the second time you

have referred to them,' said I anxiously; 'and they are—'

'That I should marry my cousin Naseby, whom I always disliked,' said Estelle in a sad and sweetly modulated voice; 'or Lord Pottersleigh, whose wealth and influence are so great that a short time must see him created an earl; but he has no chance *now*, dear Harry!'

Long, lovingly, and tenderly she gazed into my eyes, and her glance and her manner seemed so truthful and genuine that I felt all the rapture of trusting her fearlessly, and that neither time nor distance would alter or lessen her regard for me; and a thousand times in 'the distant hours' that came did I live over and over again that scene in the arbour, when the warm flush of the August evening was lying deep on the Welsh woods and mountains, when all the mullioned windows of the quaint old mansion were glittering in light, and the soft coo of the wild pigeons was heard as they winged their way to the summit of Craigaderyn, which is usually alive with them, and there the fierce hawk and the ravenous cormorant know well when to find their prey.

The time for my departure drew near, and already but a day remained to me. Caradoc and Charley Gwynne had already sailed in a troopship for Varna, from which the entire army was about to embark for a landing on the Russian coast, and ill or well, my presence with the regimental dépôt was imperative.

My bullock trunks had been packed by Owen Gwyllim, and the carriage was ordered to convey me next evening, after an early dinner. The latter passed slowly and heavily enough, and afterwards, instead of remaining all together, as might have been expected, circumstances separated us for an hour or so. Lady Naseby was indisposed; so was Lord Pottersleigh, whom his old enemy had confined by the feet to his rooms, yet he hoped to be in service order, to enact the sportsman on the coming 1st of September, a period to which he looked forward with disgust and horror, as involving an enormous amount of useless fatigue, with the chances of shooting himself or some one else. Sir Madoc had certain country business to attend; and on the three young ladies retiring to the drawing-room, I was left to think over my approaching departure through the medium of burgundy and a cigar.

My sword arm was nearly well now; but still I should have made but a poor affair of it, if compelled to resort to inside and outside cuts, to point and parry, with a burly Muscovite.

To know that I had but a few hours left me now, and not to spend them with Estelle Cressingham, seemed intolerable! Before me, from the window, spread the far extent of grassy chase steeped in the evening sunshine; above the green woods were the peaks of Snowdon and Carneydd Llewellyn, dim and blue in the distance; and while gazing at them wistfully, I reflected on all I should have to see and undergo, to hope and fear and suffer—the miles I should have to traverse by sea and land—ere I again heard, if ever, the pleasant rustle of the leaves in these old woods, the voice of the wild pigeon or the croak of the rooks among the old Tudor gables and chimneys of Craigaderyn. And then again I thought of Estelle.

'I *must* see her, and alone too, at all risks; perhaps dear little Dora will assist me,' I muttered, and went towards the drawing-room, which was now considerably involved in shadow, being on the western side of the Court; and I felt with the tender Rosalind, when her lover said, 'For these two hours, Rosalind, I will leave thee,' 'Alas, dear love, I cannot lack thee two hours.'

I entered the room and found only Winifred Lloyd. She was seated in the deep bay of a very picturesque old oriel window, which seemed to frame her as if in a picture. Her chin was resting in the hollow of her left hand, and she was gazing outward dreamily on vacancy, or along the flower-terraces of the house; but she looked hastily round, and held out a hand to me as I approached.

I caressed the pretty hand, and then dropped it; and not knowing very well what to say, leaned over the back of her chair.

'I suppose,' she began, 'you are thinking—thinking—'

'How far more pleasing to the eye are a pair of fair white shoulders to the same amount of silk or satin,' said I smilingly, as I patted her neck with my glove.

She shrugged the white shoulders in question, and said petulantly, with half averted face,

'Is it possible that your departure has no place in your thoughts?'

'Alas, yes! for do I not leave Craigaderyn by

sunset? and its golden farewell rays are lingering on blue Snowdon even now,' said I, with a forced smile; for though I had come in quest of Estelle, something—I know not what—drew me to Winifred just then.

Her eyebrows were very black, but slightly arched, and they almost met over her nose; and I gazed into the orbs below them, so dark, so clear and beautiful—eyes that could neither conceal the emotions of her heart, nor the pleasure or sorrow she felt; and I thought how easily a man might be lured to forget the world for her, as friendship between the sexes—especially in youth—is perilous; and some such thought perhaps occurred to her, for she turned her face abruptly from me.

'You are surely not angry with me?' said I, bending nearer her ear.

'Angry—I with you?'

'Yes.'

'Why should I be so?' she asked, looking down upon her folded hands that trembled in her lap,—for she was evidently repressing some emotion; thinking perhaps of poor Phil Caradoc, who was then ploughing the waters of the Mediterranean with Carneydd Llewellyn to console him.

'You should not have come here,' said she, after a pause.

'Not into the drawing-room?'

'Unless to meet Estelle Cressingham.'

'Do not say this,' said I nervously and imploringly, in a low voice; 'what is Estelle to me?'

'Indeed!' said the little scornful lip. 'Her mamma summoned her, but she may be here shortly.'

Doubtless Lady Naseby had some dread of the leave-taking.

'I shall be so glad to see her once again ere I go.'

'Of course.'

'I hope that you and she will often think and speak of me when I am gone.'

'You are a delightful egotist, Harry Hardinge; but I trust our memories may be reciprocal.'

'We have ever been such friends, and must be, you know, Winifred.'

'Yes, Harry; why should we *not* be friends?' she asked, with a dash of passionate earnestness in her tone, while she gazed at me with a curious expression in her large, soft, and long-lashed eyes.

'Have you any message for—for—'

' Whom?' she asked sharply.

' Philip Caradoc.'

' None.'

' None !'

' Save kindest regards and warmest wishes. What is Mr. Caradoc to me?' Then she gave a little shiver, as she added, ' Our conversation is taking a very strange tone.'

' I cannot conceive in how I have annoyed you,' said I, with something of sorrow and wonder in my heart.

' Perhaps; but you have not annoyed me, though you are not quite what you used to be; and none are so blind as those who will not see.'

' I am quite perplexed. I think we know each other pretty well, Winifred?' said I, very softly.

' I know you certainly,' was the dubious response.

' Well—and I you?' said I, laughing.

' Scarcely. Woman, you should be aware, is a privileged enigma.'

' Well, I was about to say that, whatever happens, we must ever be dear friends, and think of each other kindly and tenderly, for the pleasant times that are past and gone.'

'What can happen to make us otherwise?' she asked in a strange voice.

'I—may be killed,' said I, not knowing very well what to say or suggest; 'so, while there is a chance of such a contingency, let us part kindly; not so coldly as this, dear Winifred; and kiss me ere I go.'

Her lips, warm and tremulous, touched mine for an instant; but her eyes were sad and wild, and her poor little face grew ashy white as she hastened away, leaving me with Estelle, who was approaching through the long and shaded room; and when with her, Winifred Lloyd and the momentary emotion that had sprung up—emotion that I cared not and dared not *then* to analyse— were utterly forgotten.

Our interview was a very silent one. We had barely time for a few words, and heavy on my heart as lead weighed the conviction that I had to part from her—my love so recently won, so firmly promised and affianced. I knew that the days of my sojourn at Winchester must be few now; and with the chances of war before me, and temptations and aristocratic ambition left behind with her, how dubious and how remote were the chances of our meeting again!

Moments there were when I felt blindly desperate, and with my arms round Estelle.

When returning, would she still love me, as Desdemona loved her Moor, for the dangers I had dared? The days of chivalry and romance have gone; but the 'old, old story' yet remains to us, fresh as when first told in Eden.

'For life or death, for good or for evil, for weal or woe, darling Estelle, I leave my heart in your keeping!' said I, in a low passionate whisper; 'in twelve months, perhaps, I may claim you as my wife.'

'L'homme propose, et Dieu dispose,' said she quietly and tenderly. 'I yet hope to see you, were it but for a day, at Walcot Park, ere you sail.'

'Bless you for the hope your words give me!' said I, as Owen Gwyllim came to announce that the carriage was at the door, and to give me Lady Naseby's and Lord Pottersleigh's cards and farewell wishes. And from that moment all the rest of my leave-taking seemed purely mechanical; and not only Sir Madoc, his two daughters, and

Estelle, were on the terrace of the mansion to bid me adieu, but all the hearty, hot-tempered, high-cheekboned old Welsh domestics, most of whom had known me since boyhood, were also there.

The impulsive Dora brought me my courier-bag, a flask filled with brandy, and dainty sand-wiches cut and prepared by Winifred's own kind little hands (for in doing this for me she would trust neither the butler nor Mrs. Gwenny Davis the housekeeper), and then she held up her bright face to be kissed; but inspired by I know not what emotion of doubt or dread, I only touched with my lips the hands of Lady Estelle and Miss Lloyd.

Both girls stood a little apart from each other, pale as death, tremulous with suppressed emotion, and with their lashes matted and their eyes filled with tears, that pride and the presence of others restrained from falling. They were calm extern-ally, but their hearts were full of secret thoughts, to which I was long in getting the clue.

In the eyes of Estelle there was that glance or expression of loving intensity which most men have seen *once*—it may be twice—in a woman's eye, and have never, never forgotten.

Sir Madoc's brown manly hand shook mine heartily, and he clapped me on the back.

'I hope to see you yet ere you leave England, my boy, and such hopes always take the sting from an adieu,' said he, with a voice that quivered nevertheless. 'Sorry you can't stay for the 1st of September—the partridges will be in splendid order; but there is shooting enough of another kind in the preserves you are going to.'

'And may never come back from,' was the comforting addendum of old Mrs. Davis, as she applied her black-silk apron to her eyes.

'Ah, Harry,' said Sir Madoc, 'you gave a smile so like your mother just now! She was handsome; but you will never be like her, were you as beautiful as Absalom.'

'It is well that poor mamma can't hear all this,' said Dora, laughing through her tears.

'Your dear mamma, my girl, was very fond of her and of him too,' said honest Sir Madoc; and then he whispered, 'If ever you want cash, Harry, don't forget me, and Coutts and Co.—the dingy den in the Strand. Farewell—anwylbach!—good-bye!'

A few minutes more and all the tableau on the

steps had passed away. I was bowling along the tall lime avenue and down the steep mountain road, up which Phil Caradoc and I had travelled but a few weeks before.

How much had passed since *then!* and how much was inevitably to pass ere I should again see these familiar scenes!

What had I said, or left unsaid? What had I done, what had passed, or how was it, that as the train sped with me beyond brave old Chester, on and on, on and on, monotonously clanking, grinding, jarring, and occasionally shrieking, while intrenched among railway rugs, with a choice cigar between my teeth, and while I was verging into that pleasant frame of mind when soft and happy visions are born of the half-drowsy brain, lulled as it were by rapidity of motion and the sameness of recurring sounds—how was it, I say, that the strange, unfathomable expression I had seen in the soft pleading eyes of dear Winifred—distance was already making her 'dear'—mingled in my memory with the smileless, grave, and tender farewell glance of my pale Estelle; and that the sweet innocent kiss of the former was remembered with sadness and delight?

I strove to analyse my ideas, and then thrust them from me, as I lowered the carriage window and looked forth upon the flying landscape and the starry night, and muttered,

'Poor Winny—God bless her! But *two loves for one heart* will never, never do. I have been at Craigaderyn too long!'

And I pictured to myself the drawing-room there: Estelle perhaps at the piano to conceal her emotions; or listening, it might be, to the twaddle of old Pottersleigh. Winny gazing out upon the starlit terrace, trying to realise the prospect—as women proposed to will do—if she had married Phil Caradoc; or thinking of—Heaven knows what! And old Sir Madoc in his arm-chair, and dreaming, while Dora nestled by his side, of the old times, and the boy—to wit, myself—he loved so well.

END OF VOL. I.

LONDON:
ROBSON AND SONS, PRINTERS, PANCRAS ROAD, N.W.

www.ingramcontent.com/pod-product-compliance
Lightning Source LLC
Chambersburg PA
CBHW060612030726
47498CB00005B/1646